Praise for

"Balaban unleashes hilarious McGrowl. . . . Filled with absurd humor and fun, cartoonlike action."
— *USA Today,* review of
McGrowl #1: *Beware of Dog*

"Mr. Balaban takes his obvious love of language and wordplay and creates a magical tale of a mind-reading dog that all young minds should read. An intelligent and plentiful debut."
— *Jamie Lee Curtis*

"For anybody who has ever had a dog, loved a dog, or wanted a dog. A great adventure beautifully written. I hope Bob writes the next one about me."
— *Richard Dreyfuss*

Read all the books about McGrowl

#4

GOOD DOG!

Bob Balaban

AN
APPLE
PAPERBACK

SCHOLASTIC INC.
New York Toronto London Auckland Sydney
Mexico City New Delhi Hong Kong Buenos Aires

ISBN 0-439-43457-2
Copyright © 2004 by Bob Balaban

All rights reserved. Published by Scholastic Inc.
SCHOLASTIC and associated logos are trademarks and/or registered trademarks of Scholastic Inc.

10 9 8 7 6 5 4 3 2 1   4 5 6 7 8 9/0
40

Printed in the U.S.A.
First printing, March 2004

*For Tonya Rapley and
the kids at Urban Strategies*

Contents

CHAPTER ONE
Stormy Weather

Thomas Wiggins had issued strict orders forbidding McGrowl to chase the cat. But what was a self-respecting golden retriever to do? When the wiry gray feline scampered across his path, deliberately splashing mud all over him, McGrowl took off like a rocket after his speeding enemy.

It had been raining steadily for over two weeks now. The streets of Cedar Springs, Indiana, looked more like angry rivers than peaceful small-town lanes. But McGrowl didn't mind the weather. He would have gone after that cat in a hurricane.

"Let's go!" Thomas shouted. He and his best friend, Violet Schnayerson, took off after Mc-Growl as fast as their legs could carry them.

"Hurry!" Violet yelled back. "We're losing sight of him." Thomas and Violet did their best, but they knew the odds of catching up with a bionic dog chasing a cat in a raging thunderstorm were not in their favor.

Thomas could hardly be angry with Mc-Growl. He was smarter and stronger than any dog in the world. But he was still a dog. And dogs had been chasing cats since the beginning of time.

As they splashed through deep puddles of swirling mud, Thomas smiled at Violet. She smiled right back. They were cold, tired, dirty, and wet, but they were having a wonderful time. They generally did whenever McGrowl was around.

GOOD DOG!

It had been well over a year since they had discovered a lost and lonely McGrowl in a ravine on another rainy afternoon. He was the answer to countless previously unanswered prayers. Thomas had been begging for a dog ever since he had been old enough to talk. The boy's very first words were *want* and *bowwow*.

Everyone quickly came to love McGrowl. He was the unofficial mascot of Thomas's school, Stevenson Elementary. Teachers brought McGrowl apples. Students begged to take him for walks.

Thomas's brother, Roger, spent many happy hours in the backyard playing basketball with McGrowl. Roger was not known for his amazing memory, but whenever he ate out, he never forgot to bring McGrowl his leftover roast beef bones. Even Thomas's mother, Mrs. Wiggins, who never particularly cared for dogs, had come to refer fondly to McGrowl as her third son, "the one with the fur."

Mr. Wiggins, who had a lifelong fear of anything on four legs, had gotten so used to McGrowl's cheerful demeanor and gentle behavior that he'd actually patted him on one occasion. On another, Mr. Wiggins remained alone in a room with McGrowl for more than five minutes. Of course, he stood on a chair the entire time.

As Thomas and Violet raced to catch up, McGrowl finally managed to corner the cat. She hissed angrily as she bared her claws and made futile swipes at him with her drenched paws. All of a sudden, a blinding sheet of rain swept over the two enemies. When it receded, the cat was nowhere to be seen.

For a moment, McGrowl thought she had simply vanished. In truth, the cat had been knocked off her spindly legs and was being carried quickly down the street toward a storm drain.

GOOD DOG!

The drain was usually covered by a protective metal grating, but the heavy rains had washed it away, revealing a yawning, dark opening. The cat thrashed about as she fought to keep her head above the rushing current that propelled her toward it.

A crash of earsplitting thunder was followed by a flash of lightning that lit up the sky. McGrowl spotted the tip of the cat's tail just as she slipped down the drain. The raging water would carry her swiftly along a series of underground tunnels that emptied into Lake Wappinger.

Every muscle in McGrowl's powerful body quivered with anticipation, ready to spring into action. He had been chasing that cat for blocks. He wasn't about to let her get away.

"Don't do it, McGrowl!" Thomas yelled as he came rushing around the corner, Violet close behind. But McGrowl paid no attention.

He leaped into the drain after the cat and was gone in a flash.

"Head for the lake!" Thomas shouted above the rain and the thunder. "Let's hope we get there before they do." He realized that both animals would soon come hurtling out of the storm drain's tunnels into the rain-swollen waters of Lake Wappinger.

"Will he be okay?" Violet asked breathlessly. As she ran, she pulled her poncho tightly around her. It was too late. The pounding rain had already soaked her to the skin.

"Sure," Thomas replied with as much confidence as he could muster. He ordered his legs to run faster, and brushed the water from his eyes. He tried to remain calm.

True, McGrowl had bionic powers. He had X-ray vision, a shared telepathic connection with Thomas, and the strength of a hundred men. But he was, after all, a living, breathing golden retriever. The possibility that McGrowl might drown in the storm drain could not be entirely ruled out.

Meanwhile, the cat struggled to stay afloat. Bobbing up and down, she disappeared, spluttering and flailing, as McGrowl paddled closer. He watched as the cat resurfaced briefly several feet away from him, desperately shook the water from her face, and gasped for air.

Without thinking, McGrowl issued a loud "I'm coming to rescue you" bark. He plunged headlong into the murky depths and raced to save his enemy.

McGrowl hated that cat. He had spent many Saturday afternoons chasing her up trees and down alleys. But he didn't want her to die. Without the cat he loved to hate, life for McGrowl would be boring indeed.

"Are we there yet?" Violet shouted.

"I don't know, it's gotta be around here

somewhere," Thomas said as he searched nervously along the edge of the lake for the drain's outlet. "There it is!"

Thomas and Violet moved closer to the opening.

"Whatcha looking for, kids?" Officer Nelson asked suspiciously. He had been out on patrol when he noticed the two children. "You could get hurt," the policeman warned. "Don't you kids realize there's a hurricane alert?"

"We're okay, we're just waiting for my dog to come out," Thomas replied, as if dogs hurtled out of storm drains into Lake Wappinger every day. He leaned over and peered into the flood of water that gushed out of the drain and into the lake.

"You mean you have a dog in there?" Officer Nelson asked, wide-eyed.

"And a cat, too," Violet eagerly volunteered.

Officer Nelson tried to remain calm as he

switched on his walkie-talkie and hollered into it. "Help! Animals in trouble! Come quick! Mayday! Can anybody hear me?" He started running up and down, shining his flashlight in the water, searching for the missing animals.

Several residents of the tiny cottages that dotted Lake Wappinger's usually peaceful shores came out, clutching their umbrellas, to see what all the fuss was about. Giselle Flamm, who heard Officer Nelson's urgent report on her two-way radio, called her cousin, Wally, over at the local television station, WCDR. She told him to hurry on over to the lake. Something, she explained excitedly, was definitely up.

Thomas sent a quick telepathic message to McGrowl. *Are you okay?* He waited for a response. He didn't get one.

The dog was too busy to answer. He was trying to grab hold of the cat. Every time he would get close to her, the rushing current carried her out of his reach. If he didn't save her soon, the cat would be lost forever.

In a final burst of bionic strength, McGrowl's paws churned the water, and he went into hypergear. Using his powerful tail as a rudder, he sped toward the cat like an atomic submarine. In seconds, he was holding her gently in his mouth by the scruff of her limp neck, just as he had seen mother cats do with their kittens.

McGrowl and the cat came careening out of the drain and into Lake Wappinger in a tumble of water and mud and leaves — upside down and backward, but very much alive. McGrowl didn't let go of the cat for a second. He swam to the surface of the lake and quickly leaped onto the shore.

By now, Wally Flamm and his crew had arrived and were eager to document the emergency for the six o'clock news. Unfortunately,

Wally and the television cameras were pointed in the wrong direction.

"And a hush falls over the anxious crowd . . ." Wally intoned dramatically. "Will the cat and the dog survive their horrible ordeal? Or won't they? Only time will tell." He paused ominously. "At this point, the noble animals have been trapped in the drain for nearly . . ."

"Mr. Flamm, Mr. Flamm," little Molly Sissle said, tugging at his sleeve insistently.

"Quiet, please, sweetheart, we're broadcasting live," Wally whispered self-importantly.

"But, Mr. Flamm, they're over there," Molly said as she pointed at the exhausted pair. "And they're all right."

"Well, I'll be," Wally said, directing a cameraman in the direction of McGrowl, who was leaning over the bedraggled cat and prodding her gently with one of his paws.

"Oh, it's a terrible sight," Wally clucked. He was terribly nearsighted. "A vicious golden retriever, half-crazed from nearly drowning, is fighting with a poor defenseless — wait a minute . . ." Wally couldn't believe his eyes. "Quick," he ordered. "Get a close-up. This is tremendous."

He watched as McGrowl's paw pushed gently on the cat's chest and water came spurting out of her tiny mouth. Then McGrowl leaned over and carefully breathed the "breath of life" into her. He repeated the sequence several times. Finally, the cat shuddered and meowed and her eyes started rolling about. She was breathing again.

Several reporters from Cedar Springs's local paper, *Cedar Things*, had arrived to cover the calamity. They held up their cameras and flashed away.

"Oh, my golly, folks," Wally exclaimed. "The dog is doing CPR on the cat. Will you look at that! What a pooch!" As the crowd started cheering, the camera pushed in to get a better look, and Thomas reminded himself how lucky he was to have a dog like McGrowl. And then Wally Flamm made his surprising announcement.

"For bravery above and beyond the call of duty, I hereby declare this dog the recipient of station WCDR's medal of honor." Undeterred by the rain and the wind, the crowd that had gathered began cheering wildly as Wally continued. "Will the dog's rightful owner please step forward?"

Thomas was so taken aback he didn't realize Wally was talking to him. Violet gave him a gentle shove, and he lurched to the front of the crowd. "His name is Thomas Wiggins," Violet proudly announced. Then she gave his address.

Wally Flamm rushed over excitedly. "So, young man, will you tell our thousands of viewers at home what it's like to have a hero for a pet?" As he spoke, Wally aimed a large microphone at Thomas and encouraged the camera crew to move in for a close-up. Everyone started to chant: "Tho-mas! Tho-mas!"

So many flashbulbs went off it looked like the Fourth of July. The reporters leaned forward, scribbling busily on their rain-soaked notepads.

Thomas was so nervous he could barely catch his breath. At last, he opened his mouth to speak. A hush fell over the eager crowd.

"Good. It feels good," was all he could say. He looked over at McGrowl and thought he would burst with pride.

CHAPTER TWO
Special Delivery

Mrs. Wiggins was in the kitchen putting the finishing touches on the celebration dinner she was making in honor of McGrowl's daring rescue. McGrowl and the rest of the Wigginses were gathered in the den. All eyes were on the television set. The evening news was on. McGrowl was the lead story. The telephone hadn't stopped ringing all afternoon. McGrowl was a hero.

As she entered the room, Mrs. Wiggins patted the top of McGrowl's furry head and carefully placed a platter of mashed potatoes and steak, medium-well and smothered in onions, on the floor in front of him. McGrowl's favorite meal. Eating in the den was reserved for only the most special occasions.

"You did an amazing thing today, Mc-Growl." Mrs. Wiggins proudly looked down at him as she spoke. As guest of honor, he had been given his dinner before everyone else.

The dog wagged his powerful tail. He was still wrapped tightly in the cozy green bath towel Mrs. Wiggins had insisted on covering him with the minute he returned from his adventure.

"Down in front," Mr. Wiggins said. Mrs. Wiggins was blocking his view of the television set.

"Oops. Sorry, darling," she replied, and perched herself on the arm of the couch. On the television, Wally Flamm was pointing excitedly at McGrowl, who was busy saving the cat's life.

GOOD DOG!

"Where'd he ever manage to pick up CPR?" Roger asked. As he spoke, he practiced dribbling an imaginary basketball. Roger loved basketball. When he wasn't actually playing, he was thinking about playing.

"I believe it's instinctive in golden retrievers," Thomas said authoritatively. He knew this was not true, but he hoped his knowledgeable tone had convinced Roger.

There was, of course, a perfectly logical explanation why McGrowl could do many of the extraordinary things of which he was capable. He had chased the very same cat into a power plant more than a year ago. This had caused an enormous explosion, which altered every single molecule in his body.

Although McGrowl still looked like a perfectly ordinary golden retriever, he had become the world's first and only bionic dog. This was not something Thomas could share with Roger, or anyone else other than Violet.

"Wow, that's amazing," Roger replied as he tossed the imaginary ball into an imaginary hoop. Thomas breathed a sigh of relief. Roger had fallen for the lie.

"Careful of the lamp, honey, it's extremely fragile," Mrs. Wiggins said nervously as she watched Roger line up another shot.

"It's not a real basketball, Mom, it's imaginary," Roger protested.

"Well, the lamp isn't," Mrs. Wiggins said as she reached over to adjust the volume on the television.

Wally Flamm was replaying McGrowl's astonishing leap out of the water with the cat in his mouth. McGrowl only hoped that the other dogs in the neighborhood weren't watching. Saving the life of an animal his entire species despised was going to be difficult to explain. He would never live it down. He turned his big brown eyes away from the set and concentrated on his steak dinner.

GOOD DOG!

Thomas sent the dog a telepathic message: *Don't be embarrassed, boy. You did the right thing. I'm really proud of you.*

McGrowl licked the last bit of gravy from his bowl and looked gratefully at Thomas. Then he reminded the boy that he still hadn't had dessert. Thomas ran into the kitchen to bring McGrowl his treat.

Mrs. Wiggins had baked healthy dog cookies for McGrowl that looked exactly like the gooey chocolate chip ones Thomas and Roger loved. The doggie versions were made with liver bits rather than chocolate chips. Instead of flour, Mrs. Wiggins substituted textured soy protein. McGrowl hated them.

Thomas didn't have the heart to tell his mother, but after McGrowl pretended to eat the healthy cookies, Thomas would throw them out.

"Honey, can you make sure we're recording this?" Mrs. Wiggins gently asked Mr. Wiggins

as she watched Wally running over to Mc-
Growl to congratulate him. "Remember last
time the VCR was on but it didn't actually
record?"

"Have no fear," Mr. Wiggins said reassur-
ingly. "I've already double-checked the whole
thing from top to bottom. It's working like a
charm."

"Because I'd hate to miss a second of any
of this," Mrs. Wiggins added, unconvinced.

"Me, too," Thomas added as he returned
with a plate full of doggie treats. As McGrowl
pretended to nibble on one of them, Thomas
watched Wally put the big gold medal around
McGrowl's neck.

McGrowl leaned over discreetly and plugged
in the VCR, using his teeth and his large
tan nose. Poor Mr. Wiggins. He had checked
everything twice and then forgotten to plug in
the power cord.

*   *   *

GOOD DOG!

The rest of the week practically flew by. Roger scored sixteen points in the big game against Wappinger High, and he managed to pass a chemistry quiz for the first time this semester. Roger's teacher, Gosling Fletch, was so surprised he fell off his chair and twisted his ankle.

Mrs. Wiggins received a special commendation at her garden club's annual event. She created a topiary bush in the shape of McGrowl. Evelyn Pertwee, the club's esteemed chairwoman, proclaimed it the official selection at next month's national landscaping finals. Mrs. Wiggins had been walking on air ever since.

Mr. Wiggins was in particularly high spirits. Things were going well for him at the advertising agency where he worked. His new ad campaign was a hit. Happy Tooth's coconut-flavored toothpaste and mouthwash had been practically "jumping off the shelves and into the customers' arms," according to his boss, Al Lundquist. Happy Tooth was a particularly tricky brand to market since they made two lines of dental products — one for humans, one for dogs. Thanks to Mr. Wiggins, both groups of products were selling well.

Mr. Wiggins had spent many sleepless nights coming up with the Happy Tooth slogan, "Leaves your breath as soothing as a tropical breeze." In addition, he had personally designed special toothpaste-tube packaging in the shape of palm trees.

Mr. Lundquist was overjoyed with the success of the campaign. He was seriously considering assigning Mr. Wiggins the entire Happy Tooth dental products account and had mentioned this to him on more than one occasion. It was one of most important accounts in the entire advertising agency and carried with it a bonus, a promotion, and enormous prestige.

GOOD DOG!

Mr. Wiggins proudly brought home the entire Happy Tooth line of doggie products to try out on McGrowl. Thomas had to admit the dog's teeth had never looked whiter. His breath had never smelled fresher, either.

Miss Pooch thought so, too. Miss Pooch belonged to Violet's older sister, Alicia, and she followed McGrowl around whenever she had the opportunity. She was a cross between a Chihuahua and a bulldog. A bull-wawa, as Alicia liked to say.

As far as Miss Pooch was concerned, McGrowl was pretty terrific even before he started using Happy Tooth's products for dogs. His shiny white teeth and tropically fresh breath now made him doubly irresistible.

As if things weren't already going well enough, Mr. Grundy, the principal of the entire Stevenson School, declared a McGrowl Day in honor of his daring cat rescue. Thomas was allowed to bring McGrowl to all of his classes. Usually, the dog had to watch patiently from his spot outside the classroom window.

Thomas and Violet and McGrowl had decided to walk home this particular Friday afternoon. It was a lovely March day. The rain had stopped at last, and the temperature was hovering at an unseasonably comfortable fifty-five degrees. The rows of crocuses that lined the sidewalk in front of Thomas's house had raised their yellow heads in anticipation of an early spring.

All in all, things were going beautifully. Perhaps a little too beautifully. "Think they're gone for good?" Violet asked as she reached down to tie one of her shoelaces.

"If only," Thomas said wistfully. Violet didn't have to mention their names. Thomas knew immediately whom she was talking about: Milton Smudge and Gretchen Bunting. The mere thought of the evil duo filled Thomas with an uneasy dread.

McGrowl wasn't exactly crazy about them, either. During last fall's class trip to Devil's Island, Smudge and Bunting had successfully impersonated two of Stevenson's most beloved teachers, Pop Wheeler and his wife, Mamie.

They had nearly succeeded in their evil plan to kidnap McGrowl and use his superpowers to unleash a dormant volcano on the unsuspecting residents of Cedar Springs. Fortunately, Thomas, Violet, and McGrowl had stopped them at the very last minute. The duo seemed to have vanished.

But McGrowl had come to realize one important fact about the two evildoers: With Smudge and Bunting, you never knew what to expect.

On the one hand, perhaps they had perished under a pile of molten lava. On the other hand, perhaps they had survived and were currently plotting a return engagement.

Thomas and McGrowl had successfully managed to elude them. So far. But Smudge and Bunting were becoming more and more desperate. Thomas knew they would stop at nothing.

The three friends arrived at Thomas's house and started attacking the milk and cookies Mrs. Wiggins had thoughtfully arranged on the kitchen table.

"McGrowl's are on the yellow plate," Mrs. Wiggins advised as she walked over to the sink and started to do the dishes. Violet sniffed the cookie she had just picked up and put it down immediately. She had nearly eaten a liver chip cookie instead of the chocolate chip kind. "How can he eat these? They smell awful," Violet whispered to Thomas.

McGrowl sent a telepathic message to Thomas. *He doesn't. He's not stupid.*

"Oh, by the way, honey, this came for you," Mrs. Wiggins said as she casually handed Thomas an envelope. He examined it carefully. It was light purple. Vines bearing tiny green leaves were entwined around its borders. Instead of a return address, the initials E.T. were printed delicately on the back flap.

"Who's it from?" Violet asked.

"Let's have a look," Thomas said. As he started to open the envelope, McGrowl came bounding over. He sniffed at it eagerly and sent Thomas an urgent telepathic message. The letter had been written by his previous owner, a kindly old woman named Edwina Tuttle.

McGrowl was positive. His bionic nose instantly detected the distinctive odor of Edwina's lilac-scented perfume on the envelope.

Thomas quickly put down the letter and took a deep breath. He had been dreading this moment ever since McGrowl had stumbled into his life. *Does the woman want to take McGrowl back?* he wondered. He had to find out. And right away.

"Bye, Mom," Thomas said, and started for the door, with Violet and McGrowl close behind.

"But, Thomas, aren't you going to read the letter?" Mrs. Wiggins asked.

"Sure. Later. Gotta run. I promised Lenny Winkleman I'd help him with his English essay," Thomas said. "Then I'm going to Violet's." This wasn't exactly a lie. He had promised to help Lenny. But not today.

"Isn't that nice," Mrs. Wiggins said absent-mindedly as she stirred a delicious-looking pot of osso buco. She had been braising veal shanks and chopping tomatoes, onions, and herbs for more than an hour. The labor-intensive Italian stew required Mrs. Wiggins's full attention. "Dinner's at six. Don't be late."

"Can I come, too?" Violet asked. She loved

eating dinner at the Wiginses'. It was fun feeding McGrowl extra helpings under the table. It was even more fun watching Mr. Wiggins try to pretend he wasn't terrified of the golden retriever.

"Sure, honey," Mrs. Wiggins replied, adding just a pinch of turmeric to the dish, which already smelled so good McGrowl's mouth was watering. He sent Thomas a telepathic message reminding him how much he loved osso buco.

And then, Thomas, Violet, and McGrowl hurried outside to read Edwina Tuttle's letter. *She's alive!* McGrowl thought happily. He never dreamed he would hear from his previous owner. He sniffed the letter again. McGrowl could hardly believe his nose.

CHAPTER THREE
News and Clues

As Thomas and Violet and McGrowl made their way across the Wigginses' front yard and over to the sidewalk, the late afternoon sun cast a yellow glow through the trees. Thomas held up the envelope and examined it carefully.

"It's addressed to Thomas, and . . . I can't make out this next word, it got smeared," Thomas said. McGrowl poked his large tan nose close to the envelope to see for himself.

The dog had recently learned to read by peeking through the first-grade window and watching Ed Lambrakis teach his six-year-old students. Within a few days, McGrowl was able to read the entire Dick and Jane series. He strained his eyes, but unfortunately he couldn't decipher what Edwina had written, either.

Meanwhile, two pairs of beady eyes peered down at the two children and their dog through two sets of powerful microbinoculars. "They look so close I can almost taste them," Milton Smudge chuckled.

"Soon they'll be ours," Gretchen Bunting chortled.

The evil duo watched patiently from the second story of an unremarkable little house on the far side of town where the grass was seldom mowed and the trash rarely collected. They would strike again when the time was right. That time was now.

They had devised another wonderful, terrible plan to enslave McGrowl. With the bionic dog's amazing powers at their disposal, they would soon be capable of destroying Cedar Springs. And then the world — unless Thomas and McGrowl could stop them first.

McGrowl and Violet listened attentively as Thomas, still inspecting the envelope, spoke at last. "I think it says Alvin. Who's Alvin?"

McGrowl barked gently and sent Thomas a telepathic message.

"Guess his name used to be Alvin," Thomas said.

"I like McGrowl better," Violet said.

"Me, too," Thomas offered.

Me, three, McGrowl thought. And then he felt a sudden chill in the mid-March air, and his nose twitched briskly. Something was out there. But what? McGrowl couldn't put his paw on it, but whatever it was sent a quiver of uneasiness through him and shifted all his senses into high alert.

Thomas took out the letter, unfolded it, and began to read.

GOOD DOG!

March 1

Dear Thomas Wiggins,

It is with the greatest pleasure that I put pen to paper and write this letter to you. I had all but given up hope of ever seeing my wonderful Alvin again when I happened to catch his daring cat rescue on the six o'clock news. Please tell him I miss him terribly and often wonder how he is doing. Incidentally, I was thrilled to see what a magnificent job you have done taking care of my delightful pet. He looked a bit overweight but quite happy.

As Thomas stopped to turn the page, Mc-Growl sent him an indignant telepathic message. "What's he saying?" Violet asked, trying not to feel left out. She wished she could communicate telepathically with McGrowl. She occasionally attempted to practice on Miss Pooch, without much success.

"He's saying not to pay attention to Edwina.

He says television puts ten pounds on everyone." Thomas smiled as he leaned over and patted McGrowl's belly. "Don't worry, boy, I'm not gonna put you on a diet."

McGrowl breathed a sigh of relief. Thomas continued to read. He wasn't sure why, but something about the letter was making him extremely nervous.

I first encountered Alvin in a supermarket parking lot. He was tied to a fence and he had a sign around his neck. It said: "My name is Alvin. I'm gentle. I'm housebroken. Take me home. I don't eat very much." As you undoubtedly know by now, this last part is far from true. But who in their right mind would ever have taken him in if they knew how much he loved to eat?

I took Alvin home immediately, and we didn't spend a moment apart for several years, at which point I became terribly ill and had to be rushed to the hospital for emergency surgery. I don't remember anything that happened after that. I do know that when I recovered and returned home, Alvin was nowhere to be found, and I was heartbroken.

Please tell Alvin my operation was a complete success and I feel well enough to care for him once again. Please return my dog to me at your earliest convenience. I will be happy to repay you for any expenses you may incur.

Very truly yours,
Edwina Tuttle

PS: I have moved to be closer to my sister. I now live at: 7~~~~~~~~~~~~~~~~~~~~~~~~~~

Poor Thomas. He couldn't believe what he had just read. Life without McGrowl was unimaginable. But, of course, Edwina had every right to ask for her own dog back. And if McGrowl wanted to return to Edwina, Thomas would never stand in the way of his happiness.

Thomas did his best to smile as he reached down to pat McGrowl. "Isn't that wonderful, boy!" McGrowl wagged his tail and looked up at Thomas expectantly, as if to say, "Please, can we go see Edwina now?" Which was, in fact, precisely what he was thinking.

Thomas gave Violet a quick but meaningful glance. The glance let her know exactly what was on Thomas's mind. She nodded back. Violet couldn't imagine life without McGrowl, either. Sometimes best friends had a psychic connection, too. Not just boys and their bionic dogs.

McGrowl sent his boy a telepathic message: *Don't worry. Although I miss Edwina and would enjoy visiting with her, my real home is with you now.*

Thomas was grateful and relieved. But would

McGrowl feel the same way once he was actually reunited with his former owner? That was a chance Thomas would have to take.

At last he spoke. "We're gonna take McGrowl to visit Edwina Tuttle."

McGrowl jumped up on Thomas and wagged his tail so forcefully he sent a nearby trash can flying and nearly blew down a small elm tree. "Easy, boy," Thomas said.

"How will we ever find her?" Violet asked. "The ink smudge blotted out her address."

"We'll find a way. We've got to," Thomas said in a quiet but determined voice. When Thomas decided to do something, nothing could stand in his way. And then, the matter resolved, he picked up a stick and threw it as far as he could. "Fetch, boy," he said as McGrowl prepared to leap into action.

"Uh-oh," Violet warned as she noticed the stick heading across the street, right toward Elsie Nugent's front window.

Thomas saw a blur of yellow whizzing by, accompanied by a powerful gust of wind and a whooshing sound. The next minute the stick was sitting at his feet, and McGrowl was looking at him eagerly. He wasn't even out of breath. In less than a second, McGrowl prevented Elsie's window from getting broken and Thomas from getting grounded.

"Brings new meaning to the words *good dog*," Violet said, grinning.

"Sure does," Thomas added as he ruffled the fur on McGrowl's flanks. "We're going to Violet's house to make a plan, McGrowl. Wanna come?" McGrowl barked happily.

"We are?" Violet said, surprised. And then she quickly added, "I mean, we are. Of course we are." Violet loved it when Thomas and McGrowl came over to her house. Usually it was the other way around. At the Wigginses' house something mouthwateringly delicious was always baking or frying or roasting in the oven.

This was not often the case at Violet's house. As Mrs. Schnayerson was fond of saying, "If mothers were meant to be cooks, they would have been given wooden spoons instead of hands."

Thomas wasn't hungry. He had more important matters on his mind. In two minutes, they were at Violet's house, looking up *Tuttle, Edwina,* in the phone book. The name was nowhere to be found. They tried calling the three other Tuttles they found there. William and Lester didn't answer. Harriet did, but she had never heard of Edwina.

In the meantime, Mrs. Schnayerson disappeared into the den to work on "Mother Knows Best," her weekly advice column in the local paper, *Cedar Things.*

"Maybe we should do an Internet search for her," Violet suggested. "My computer's in the bedroom."

But again, no Edwina Tuttle was to be found

anywhere in the vicinity. They did manage to locate an Edwina Tuttle in Maryland and an E. Tuttle in Alaska. But the envelope carrying the letter bore no stamp and no visible post-mark. Apparently, it had been hand-delivered. Edwina Tuttle had clearly not come all the way to Indiana from Maryland or Alaska to deliver a letter.

"No," Thomas decided, "she must live somewhere around here."

He dialed Directory Assistance. "Maybe it's a new number and it isn't in the phone book yet," Thomas suggested. But the operator found no new listings for any Tuttle, Edwina or otherwise.

"Think we should dust the letter for finger-prints?" Violet asked hopefully. She had re-ceived a home fingerprint analysis set for Christmas and was eager to use it.

"I'm not really sure how that would help," Thomas replied. And then he noticed a round brownish spot at the bottom of the letter. "Wait a minute. What's this?" Thomas wondered. McGrowl came over and analyzed the spot with his X-ray vision. It turned out to be a dead ant and was of no use whatsoever in locating Edwina.

Then the phone rang. Mrs. Schnayerson picked it up. A moment later she called up to the children. "Thomas, your mother says you're late for dinner. Violet, honey, you forgot to tell me you were eating at the Wigginses' tonight. McGrowl, it looks like you're the only one here who isn't in the doghouse."

McGrowl, Violet, and Thomas said a quick good-bye to Mrs. Schnayerson and hurried across the street and down the block to the Wigginses' house. The doghouse wasn't a place in which Thomas especially wanted to remain.

CHAPTER FOUR
The Cat Came Back

As Thomas, Violet, and McGrowl approached the house, McGrowl smelled something and instinctively began to growl. His ears stood up and he looked around nervously.

"What's the matter, boy?" Thomas asked. And then he noticed the object of McGrowl's concern. Sitting right on the front doorstep, looking as if she belonged there, was the cat McGrowl loved to hate.

She appeared to be fully recovered from her experience in the storm drain and had dropped by to thank her noble rescuer.

GOOD DOG!

Before Thomas could stop him, McGrowl started racing for the cat as fast as he could. Instead of running in the opposite direction as she usually did, the cat didn't budge an inch. McGrowl screeched to a halt to avoid running into her. His claws dug a path of destruction about three feet long right down the middle of Mrs. Wiggins's perfect front lawn.

This was not the way it was supposed to be. Dogs chased cats. Cats ran. Period. End of subject. McGrowl was so confused he forgot to be mad.

Thomas figured it out immediately. His suspicions were confirmed when the cat rubbed her back against McGrowl's leg and started purring. The cat liked McGrowl. No, the cat *loved* McGrowl. McGrowl had saved her life. She was grateful. The cat was McGrowl's new best friend.

McGrowl read Thomas's mind and his eyes widened in dismay. He barked loudly and gave the cat his most menacing expression. The cat jumped on his back and started rubbing her whiskers against his neck. McGrowl was mortified. The cat was crazy about him.

Then Mrs. Wiggins appeared in the doorway, wiping her hands on a dish towel and tapping her foot. "You're forty minutes late, the osso buco's burned to a crisp, and I have no idea where your father is." She was trying to remain calm. She wasn't having much success.

"Strange," Mrs. Wiggins muttered when she saw the cat sitting on McGrowl's back. "Very strange." And then she noticed the large, jagged furrow in her precious lawn. "You're going to have a lot of explaining to do, young man," she said sternly to Thomas just as Alicia arrived with Miss Pooch in her arms.

Alicia had a study date with Roger. They had a chemistry final tomorrow, and Roger was having trouble memorizing the periodic table. Alicia decided to bring Miss Pooch along for the evening. She knew how much the bullwawa liked McGrowl. Miss Pooch was thrilled. She was looking forward to some special time alone with the dog of her dreams.

McGrowl barked happily at the sight of Miss Pooch. He enjoyed spending time with the funny-looking dog with the big personality. Miss Pooch took one look at the cat sitting on McGrowl's back and leaped out of Alicia's arms. She was jealous. As far as Miss Pooch was concerned, riding on McGrowl's back was a privilege reserved for her and her alone.

Without a moment's hesitation, the bullwawa jumped up on McGrowl and started yipping at the cat and batting her ineffectively with her tiny front paws. This was met with a flurry of screeches, hisses, barks, yowls, and general mayhem.

"Naughty, Miss Pooch! Naughty!" Alicia screamed to no avail. Miss Pooch never listened to anybody.

McGrowl tried to buck the cat off his shoulders while Miss Pooch yipped and jumped. The cat bared her teeth and swiped at Miss Pooch with her sharp claws. The left corner of Mrs. Wiggins's rhododendron patch was already in shreds, and one of her favorite hydrangeas had fallen victim to the onslaught.

Thomas concentrated with all his might. *Calm down, McGrowl. I mean it! You're in big trouble.* McGrowl paid absolutely no attention to the telepathic warnings. He was having far too much fun.

Meanwhile, Mrs. Wiggins attempted to shoo the cat away by waving a dish towel at her. This only seemed to intensify the cat's determination. Alicia gave up trying to control Miss

Pooch and disappeared into the house to look for Roger.

At that very moment, Mr. Wiggins came strolling proudly down the street with his boss, Al Lundquist, at his side. Mr. Lundquist had finally decided to award Mr. Wiggins the entire Happy Tooth dental products account. In an outburst of uncharacteristic spontaneity, Mr. Wiggins had invited him and his wife to dinner. Mrs. Lundquist would be arriving shortly. Unfortunately, in all the excitement, Mr. Wiggins had neglected to let Mrs. Wiggins in on the plans.

As Mr. Wiggins and his guest arrived at the house, Mrs. Wiggins removed her apron, smoothed her hair, and prayed that the animals would stop fighting. Then she ran over to say hello.

Mr. Wiggins couldn't take his eyes off what appeared to be a small furry tornado whirling about the front yard. Dust and dying weeds were flying. It was all he could do not to run screaming into the house. His heart pounded. His face turned red. He clenched his fists.

And then Mr. Wiggins thought about his new account and everything that came with it. He thought about his new corner office. He thought about his promotion and his new title, executive vice president. He thought about his bonus.

Before he realized what he was doing, he had pulled himself up to his fullest height, stuck out his chin, and bellowed, "That's enough, everyone stop this nonsense right now!" in a voice that caused even the birds in the trees to stop twittering and come to attention. Much to everyone's surprise, McGrowl, Miss Pooch, and the cat stopped fighting. They all looked over at Mr. Wiggins, stunned.

The silence was deafening. Mrs. Wiggins and Mr. Lundquist stared at Mr. Wiggins in amazement. Thomas and Violet held their breath. No one dared move. But Miss Pooch was furious. She was convinced that if Mr. Wiggins hadn't come along and broken up the fight, she would have beaten the cat and reestablished herself as McGrowl's number one admirer.

She summoned every ounce of energy she could muster and hurled herself onto Mr. Wiggins's head.

At first Mr. Wiggins decided to pretend that nothing was happening. It did feel an awful lot like a dog was sitting on his head. But if he couldn't see it, perhaps it wasn't really there. He stood immobile, praying that whatever was digging its claws into his scalp would go away.

Meanwhile, Mrs. Wiggins tried to distract Mr. Lundquist with casual banter. "Lovely weather, isn't it?" she began.

"Oh, yes," Al Lundquist replied.

"I can't remember a nicer third week of March," Mrs. Wiggins gushed.

"That's so interesting," Lundquist volunteered. He wasn't really paying attention. He was busy trying not to stare at Mr. Wiggins, who was busy trying not to scream.

"Uh-huh," Mrs. Wiggins replied. She wasn't really paying attention, either. She was stealing nervous glances at Mr. Wiggins, who was starting to shake. A nervous, moaning sound escaped from his tightly closed mouth.

"Honey, would you care for a mint?" It was the only thing Mrs. Wiggins could think of to say.

Mr. Wiggins stared, wide-eyed, back at her. Clearly he was about to lose control. "Mmm-mint? Mmmmint?" he stammered, and suddenly took off. He practically flew down the street as he tried to shake Miss Pooch off his head. He nearly ran over Dot Lundquist, who had just pulled up and was trying to decide whether to get out of her car.

Miss Pooch waited until Mr. Wiggins ran

past the Schnayerson house and then hopped off his head as if Mr. Wiggins was a bus delivering her to her doorstep. In a flash, she was prancing through her doggie door and into her house.

McGrowl sheepishly surveyed the mess in the front yard while the cat looked coyly down at him from a low branch of a nearby tree. She was leaving, but she would be back.

When Mrs. Wiggins finally spoke, she put on her most cheerful voice. "Would anybody care for a drink?"

"Yes!" cried the Lundquists. A little too quickly, and a little too loud.

CHAPTER FIVE
Something's Cooking

Several uneasy minutes had passed and Mr. Wiggins had yet to return. Mrs. Wiggins and the Lundquists were sitting in the living room sipping tall glasses of iced tea with little umbrellas in them, while Thomas, Violet, and McGrowl passed around hors d'oeuvres.

Mrs. Wiggins had taken the news that the Lundquists were staying for dinner surprisingly well. She quickly whipped up some tasty appetizers from leftover lobster salad, lettuce wedges, and anything else she could find in the vegetable crisper.

GOOD DOG!

McGrowl served from a small tray he carefully balanced on his back. He insisted on having Thomas tie a checkered dish towel jauntily around his neck. He had seen a waiter in a French bistro on TV wear the same thing.

"I'll have another one of those delicious whatchamacallits, if you don't mind," Mr. Lundquist said as he grabbed another fistful of the appetizers.

"What *do* you call them?" Dot Lundquist asked, taking one herself. "They're beyond good."

"I call them . . . *whatchamacallits*," Mrs. Wiggins said brightly.

"Well," Dot Lundquist said, reaching for another one, "you are not getting me out of this house without the recipe for those whatdayacallems. I cannot keep my hands off them."

So far Mrs. Wiggins was earning high marks for food. What she would do for the rest of the meal, however, remained a mystery.

"I can't wait to see what's for dinner," Al Lundquist said, patting his large round belly in anticipation.

"Me, too," Mrs. Wiggins chirped gaily as she rose from her seat. "Thomas, honey, could I see you in the kitchen for a moment?" she said, casually wiping up some crumbs from the coffee table. As she leaned over, she whispered urgently into his ear. "On the double, mister, and bring McGrowl."

"Sure, Mom," Thomas replied equally casually, and then raced into the kitchen, with Mc-Growl at his heels.

While the Lundquists and Violet waited in the living room, Mrs. Wiggins issued orders. Thomas and McGrowl stood at attention in front of the stove.

"Thomas, you chop the broccoli and dice the carrots," she spoke softly and quickly. "When you're finished, beat five egg whites until foamy. Go." Thomas ran to the refrigerator.

GOOD DOG!

"McGrowl, I'm calling the butcher. Pick up six chicken breasts, skinless, boneless, and lightly pounded. Make sure they're fresh. Hurry." In a second, Mrs. Wiggins was on the phone placing her order, Thomas was chopping away, and McGrowl was halfway to the butcher.

Fortunately, Mrs. Wiggins was in such a rush it never occurred to her that a golden retriever had understood every word she said and was running an errand well beyond the capabilities of a normal dog. Before she could give the matter a moment's thought, McGrowl was back with the chicken.

Mr. Wiggins returned a few minutes later. Miraculously, the chicken breasts had been sauteed and the vegetables had been diced. The house was filled with the sugary smell of a freshly baking cake.

Mr. Wiggins had run nearly a mile before he noticed Miss Pooch was no longer on his head. Then he had run back. He was exhausted and disheveled. As he entered, he waved feebly to the guests. He was panting so hard he couldn't speak. The Lundquists were so busy eating the few remaining whatchamacallits they barely noticed him.

Then Mrs. Wiggins hurried into the living room and rang the little crystal bell Mr. Wiggins had given her for their tenth anniversary. She greeted her husband with a cheery "Welcome back" and uttered three of McGrowl's favorite words, *"Diner est servi."*

"That's French for *dinner is served*," Violet graciously explained. Everyone moved into the dining room. McGrowl came in once everyone was seated, pulling a small serving cart with his teeth. It was filled to the brim with platters of delicious-looking food.

"Anybody ever hear the one about the dentist and the man from Mars?" Mr. Wiggins asked hopefully as Mrs. Wiggins passed the food to the guests. Evidently, he had recovered sufficiently from his ordeal to tell one of his infamous bad jokes.

A muffled groan emerged from under the table. Even McGrowl hated Mr. Wiggins's jokes.

"Spare us, Wiggins. That one's so old it's got whiskers." Al Lundquist laughed as he dug into an enormous portion of chicken breasts Wigginaise. "Looks so good, I hate to eat it."

Then don't, McGrowl thought. *More leftovers for the rest of us.*

As Mrs. Wiggins passed around the sauce for the broccoli-carrot puree, Dot Lundquist looked up happily. "I don't believe I've ever tasted better chicken. What's your secret?"

Mrs. Wiggins lowered her voice and leaned in close to Mrs. Lundquist as if she were di-

vulging classified information. "Prepare everything at the very last minute," she replied.
"Holds in the flavor."

"What song did the decaying tooth sing in
the church choir?" Mr. Wiggins asked, undeterred by the lack of enthusiasm for his previous joke. In honor of his promotion, Mr. Wiggins
had decided to confine himself entirely to
jokes about teeth.

"Holy, holy, holy," Mr. Lundquist replied
through a mouth full of what Mrs. Wiggins re-
ferred to as "two-minute potatoes." In truth,
she had only had time to make one-minute
potatoes. The Lundquists didn't care. They
were eating up a storm. If the jokes weren't
going well, the food portion of the evening
certainly was.

At last, Mr. Lundquist rapped on his glass
with his fork, and the table grew silent. "I'm
proud of you, Henry Wiggins. Your work on

the Happy Tooth campaign so far has been extraordinary. I expect great things from you." Everyone applauded.

A tear glistened in the corner of Mrs. Wiggins's eye, and she looked lovingly over at her husband. "I'm so happy, honey. I'd love you even if you weren't executive vice president of the entire Happy Tooth new products account." Everyone applauded some more. Mrs. Wiggins hurried into the kitchen to dry her eyes and bring in the dessert.

"Lights out, please!" she called from the kitchen. McGrowl turned off the switch with one of his big floppy paws. The room was plunged into darkness.

A moment later, Mrs. Wiggins emerged, bearing her wondrous creation. Somehow she had managed to throw together a mouthwatering three-layer cake complete with vanilla buttercream frosting and raspberry jam filling.

The cake was shaped like an enormous tooth. And not just any tooth. It was an anatomically correct version of a rear lower molar, exactly thirty times larger than scale, festooned with sparklers and rainbow sprinkles. The gentle glow from the sparklers twinkled and shone throughout the room.

Mrs. Wiggins began to sing. "Happy too-ooth to you . . ."

Everybody joined in. "Happy too-ooth to you . . . Happy too-ooth, dear Henry, happy too-ooth to you." McGrowl howled from underneath the table.

Henry Wiggins leaned over and blew out all of the sparklers with one enormous breath. And then he rose and began to speak. "First of all, I'd like to thank my wonderful wife for making this amazing tooth cake." Mrs. Wiggins smiled sweetly. "It's as realistic as it is thoughtful. And that's saying a lot."

Mrs. Wiggins's face flushed with happiness.

Mr. Wiggins continued. "I'd also like to thank Al Lundquist" — he paused dramatically — "for believing in me." He lifted his glass to Mr. Lundquist. "And for giving me this tremendous opportunity. I can't tell you what it means to me." Al Lundquist beamed proudly and lifted his glass in return.

"And last but not least, I'd like to thank tooth decay." Everyone looked at Mr. Wiggins as if he were out of his mind. He continued, undaunted. "Because if we didn't have tooth decay, we wouldn't need Happy Tooth products, and I'd be out of a job."

Everyone began to laugh. Mr. Wiggins had made a joke. And it was actually funny. Even Mrs. Wiggins had to chuckle, and she never laughed at her husband's jokes.

Everyone raised his or her glass high in the air. McGrowl thumped his tail loudly on the floor. Above the table, glasses clinked merrily and a resounding chorus of "Cheers!" echoed throughout the room.

Thomas was enormously pleased for his father's success. But try as he might, he couldn't stop thinking about Edwina's letter and the disturbing possibility of giving up Mc-Growl.

CHAPTER SIX
Back to Business

"Where do we begin?" Violet asked. "We can't just go around knocking on every door in Cedar Springs."

Thomas looked up from Edwina's letter. He was studying it for clues. "I don't know. But I'll think of something."

Thomas and Violet and McGrowl had helped with the dishes, then they went upstairs to Thomas's room. Thomas's parents and the Lundquists sat in the living room consuming endless cups of after-dinner coffee.

McGrowl paced back and forth nervously.

All he could think of tonight was locating Edwina. "We'll find her, boy. I promise," Thomas said gently. McGrowl padded over to the window and looked out sadly.

The Lundquists were finally leaving. But not before Mr. Lundquist had eaten everything in sight, including the sugar cubes Mrs. Wiggins had put out with the coffee. At one point, Mr. Wiggins feared he was going to eat the candles.

"Look harder," Violet said. "There's gotta be a clue in there somewhere." Thomas held the envelope up to the lamp on his desk and scrutinized it intensely, using the powerful magnifying glass that came with his Butterflies of the World kit. "Any luck?" she asked.

Thomas wasn't listening. He bit his lower lip and furrowed his brow. He didn't say anything for a long time. He twisted and turned the letter and held it so close to the light that Violet was worried it might catch on fire. "Wait a minute. I think I see something," he said at last.

Thomas had noticed a series of indistinct markings pressed into the back of the envelope. Evidently, Edwina had been scribbling a note to herself, and the envelope had been resting underneath the paper upon which she had been writing. But the markings were so faint Thomas couldn't make them out.

McGrowl rushed over to look. He sent Thomas a telepathic message. "McGrowl says he sees something, too," Thomas told an excited Violet. "And he thinks he can decipher it. What is it, boy?"

McGrowl concentrated with all his might. His microscopic vision carefully scanned every fiber of the delicate piece of paper. One by one a series of numbers came into focus.

"Don't forget to floss, son," Mr. Wiggins called in from the other room. "And help McGrowl brush his teeth."

Thomas wasn't listening. He was concentrating on the telepathic message he was receiving from McGrowl.

Five . . . two . . . six . . . McGrowl sent Thomas numbers and Thomas wrote them down, until ten digits were staring him right in the face.

And then, he realized. "It's a phone number! And an area code."

"Whose?" Violet asked.

"I have no idea," Thomas answered. "Edwina was probably calling someone, and she must have written down the number." By now, Thomas was halfway down the stairs and on his way to the kitchen. He could use the telephone there unobserved. McGrowl and Violet followed close behind.

"Maybe if we find the person she was calling, he or she can help us find her," Violet said.

"That's the plan," Thomas answered, opening the door to the kitchen.

Unfortunately, Mrs. Wiggins was still washing the counters and repotting several orchids in preparation for next year's flower and garden show. They would find no privacy there.

"Don't make a mess," she said, not looking up. "The kitchen's clean."

"I just wanted to thank you for a lovely dinner, Mrs. Wiggins," Violet said, thinking quickly as she headed for the back door. "I'm going home now."

"McGrowl and I are gonna walk her," Thomas added. They would use the telephone at Violet's.

In a minute, Thomas, Violet, and McGrowl were at the Schnayersons', getting ready to dial the mysterious phone number. Violet's parents were busy in the den playing canasta with their cousins Bette and Mitch Kowalski.

Thomas dialed the numbers from the envelope slowly and with great care. Five . . .

two . . . six . . . two . . . two . . . one . . . seven . . . three . . . four . . . two.

McGrowl stood by the phone and pressed his ear close to the receiver. He didn't want to miss a word. As he waited for it to ring, he thought about how much he had missed Edwina and the smell of her lilac perfume. The phone was ringing now. It rang seven or eight long rings. Wasn't anybody home?

Thomas was about to give up when he heard the receiver on the other end being picked up. And then dropped. And then a lot of fumbling could be heard as the phone was picked up and dropped several more times. At one point it actually sounded as if someone was kicking it around the room. The activity was accompanied by strenuous grunting and heavy breathing. It occurred to Thomas that perhaps a wild animal of some kind had knocked the receiver off its cradle and was playing with it.

GOOD DOG!

At last, an ancient voice began to speak. It was a man's voice. It quivered and trembled and shook. "Where the dickens are you, Maudie, you old bat! You're never around when I need you," the voice complained to an unseen friend. Or enemy.

Apparently, the man was having difficulty merely holding on to the phone. He panted heavily. The act of picking up the receiver seemed to be taxing him unbearably. "Hello! Hello!" He shouted feebly, as if this were the first time he had ever used a telephone.

"Say something," Violet urged, "or he'll hang up and die before we have a chance to speak to him."

"This is Thomas Wiggins," Thomas began.

"There's . . . no . . . Thomas . . . Wiggins . . . here." The old man took enormous pauses between every word.

"No, *this* is Thomas Wiggins,"

"What are ya, deaf? I already told ya

there's . . . no . . . Thomas . . . Wiggins . . . here." The man was becoming increasingly agitated. Thomas heard more struggling. Someone was attempting to wrench the phone out of the old man's hands. Thomas could hear muffled cursing and shouting. At last, a soothing female voice could be heard.

"This is the residence of Wilbur Foote. I am his caregiver, Maude Simple. To whom do I have the pleasure of speaking?"

"My name is Thomas Wiggins," Thomas said, much relieved, "and I'm looking for Edwina Tuttle."

"You don't say," Maude Simple replied. "I knew the woman well."

McGrowl's heart skipped a beat.

"Do you have any idea where she is?" Thomas asked.

"That's a good question," Miss Simple replied. "I haven't heard from her in quite a while. Wilbur still hears from her occasionally."

"That's wonderful," Thomas said. McGrowl's ears perked up.

"No, it isn't," the woman answered dryly. "They don't get along very well. He's her oldest living relative, you know."

"I had no idea."

"He'll be a hundred and four years old next week." *No wonder he had so much trouble holding on to the receiver,* Thomas thought.

"Of course, Edwina wouldn't tell you her age if her life depended on it," Maude Simple added.

"Do you think Mr. Foote could tell me where Edwina is?" Thomas wondered.

"Maybe. But he won't tell you anything over the telephone. Doesn't trust it. Never has. Doesn't much care for the automobile, either. But that's Wilbur Foote for ya."

After much negotiating, Maude finally got Wilbur to agree to meet briefly with Thomas and Violet tomorrow — as long as they made sure to arrive sometime after his morning nap and before his afternoon nap. Evidently, Wilbur spent a great part of the day asleep. She gave Thomas Wilbur's address: 126½ Round Swamp Lane.

At this point, the old man started screeching at Maude and attempted to regain control of the telephone. Thomas quickly thanked Maude and hung up the phone at last.

"Time to go home, Thomas," Mrs. Schnayerson called from the den. She was on a winning streak and didn't want to leave the table. Mrs. Schnayerson and Mrs. Wiggins belonged to a secret club for mothers devoted to getting one another's children back home at a reasonable hour.

"Sure, Mrs. Schnayerson," Thomas yelled back. He and Violet agreed to get together first thing in the morning. Thomas and Mc-Growl were home and washed and ready for bed before Thomas's mother could say, "Clean your closet."

McGrowl curled up peacefully at the foot of the bed. Thomas reached down and scratched the itchy place on the back of his neck, right behind his collar. Thomas always knew just where to scratch.

Thomas didn't fall asleep right away. He tossed and he turned as he thought about his impending journey. A journey that might eventually lead to Edwina Tuttle. He wondered what she would look like. He wondered where she lived. He wondered if he would like her as much as McGrowl seemed to like her. He wondered if he would have to give Mc-Growl back to her.

Soon enough, Thomas was snoring. Mc-Growl yawned and turned over quietly. He was careful not to awaken the boy. The dog was having trouble falling asleep. He was thinking about Milton Smudge and Gretchen Bunting. It wasn't like them to remain out of the picture for so long.

They would be back. McGrowl could feel it in his bones. He could sense their evil presence in the cold night air. Until they were gone for good, McGrowl would sleep with one eye open.

The wind whistled through the trees, and a full moon cast dancing shadows on the curtains. A dog could be heard barking in the distance. McGrowl recognized the high, yippy sound. It was Miss Pooch. She was refusing to go to bed. He thought about how much he looked forward to seeing the bullwawa again. He pictured her pointy teeth and her funny ears. He thought about her scruffy coat and her cute little undershot chin. He sighed contentedly.

GOOD DOG!

And in a minute McGrowl was fast asleep. Mrs. Wiggins could hear his snoring all the way down the hall. She smiled as she turned out the light beside her bed and thought about how lucky she was to have a dog like McGrowl watching over her boy.

CHAPTER SEVEN
On the Road

"Breakfast is in five minutes," Mrs. Wiggins called from the kitchen. "And I want those hands scrubbed, young man. Flu season is still upon us."

Thomas looked up and nodded in absent-minded agreement. He was in his room, preparing for the day ahead. His backpack was already bulging with all sorts of things he thought might come in handy during his search for Edwina.

Don't forget your magic rock, McGrowl reminded him.

GOOD DOG!

Thomas's mother had given it to him, just as her mother had given it to her when she was a little girl. Mrs. Wiggins said it would keep Thomas safe from harm, and so far it had seemed to. Thomas never liked to embark on an adventure without it.

Thanks, he thought as he went to his dresser and took out the rock from its special place in his sweater drawer. He tucked it into his pocket and patted it a couple of times to remind himself that it was there.

McGrowl went to the closet and picked up his special comb and brush with his teeth. He walked over to Thomas, dropped them at his feet, and refused to budge until Thomas combed out all his tangles and brushed his smooth thick fur until it shone. He wanted to make sure he looked his very best for Edwina.

"Acknowledgment, please," Mrs. Wiggins said as she knocked softly and opened the door to Thomas's bedroom. McGrowl gave a cheerful, attentive bark that let her know both he and Thomas would be in the kitchen in a minute.

"Thank you very much," she replied, and went back downstairs to flip her perfectly round half-dollar pancakes. Since McGrowl had come to live with the Wigginses, Thomas's mother had come to understand a whole variety of his special sounds.

McGrowl sent Thomas a telepathic message. He told him to finish packing and scrub his hands. He was starving.

"So when is this science project due, son?" Mr. Wiggins asked from behind the Saturday paper. Thomas had told his parents he planned to spend the day with Violet, working on an assignment for science class. "Coffee's delicious by the way, honey."

"Well, aren't you kind, dear," Mrs. Wiggins replied. "Touch of vanilla."

"It's due next week," Thomas replied.

"What exactly are you and Violet working on, Thomas?" Mrs. Wiggins asked as she brought a platter to the table. Mounds of pancakes dripping with maple syrup were surrounded by stacks of bacon and sausage. *Please,* McGrowl thought, *let there be enough for me.* He began to whimper softly.

"Noses off the table, please," Mrs. Wiggins warned. Poor McGrowl. In his excitement he had rested his big brown nose right on the edge of the platter.

McGrowl didn't need to be asked twice. He backed away from the table immediately and lay down quietly at his place on the floor beside Thomas's chair.

"Thank you, McGrowl," Mrs. Wiggins said quietly. As a special treat, she leaned down and gave McGrowl his very own bowl of pancakes and sausages. His tail thumped happily and loudly on the floor.

"Rocks. We're collecting rocks," Thomas said in response to his mother's question.

"Rocks can be fun," Mr. Wiggins said absentmindedly as he poured an extra dollop of maple syrup onto his stack of pancakes.

"Make sure you're home on time tonight, Thomas," Mrs. Wiggins said as she flipped another batch of pancakes. "Roger's got an important basketball game in Ferndale, and we'll have to be in the car by six if we want to beat the traffic."

"Interesting," Mr. Wiggins said as he attempted to wipe a glob of syrup off his new shirt. He wasn't really listening. He was busy thinking about how excited he was to be the account executive in charge of the entire Happy Tooth dental products account.

McGrowl noticed the cat before he and Thomas were even out the door. Her distinctive scent caused his nose to pucker and his ears to perk up. Maybe he would have time for one good chase on the way to Violet's house. But when the cat noticed McGrowl, she rolled over on her back and began purring sweetly. McGrowl barked and did his best to sound menacing. The cat paid no attention.

Inside the house, Mr. Wiggins heard the noise and ran up to the bedroom to hide in the closet. He was still traumatized from his encounter with Miss Pooch the previous evening. Meanwhile, the cat started running toward McGrowl.

McGrowl sent Thomas a telepathic message: *We've got to get away from here.*

"Last one to Violet's is a rotten egg," Thomas shouted as the two friends ran as fast as they could.

How odd, Mr. Wiggins thought. He had emerged from his hiding place in the closet and was watching Thomas and McGrowl from the safety of his bedroom window. "I thought dogs were supposed to chase cats. Not the other way around." The cat was running after McGrowl as fast as her little legs could carry her.

Thomas and McGrowl picked up Violet at her house, then went to the bus stop and waited for the number five bus that would take them to Upper Wappinger and Wilbur Foote's house. McGrowl looked up and down anxiously. He was worried the cat had followed him.

Instead of the cat, he spotted Sophie Morris heading toward them and tried to warn Thomas. But it was too late. Sophie was already hurrying over to see what they were up to.

Sophie was the bossiest girl in the fifth grade, and also the nosiest. She needed to know everything that was going on with everyone at all times. And then she had to tell them what to do about it.

"Where are you guys going?" she asked.

"Upper Wappinger," Thomas answered, wishing she would go away. He didn't feel like telling the biggest gossip in the lower school he was out looking for McGrowl's original owner when his parents thought he was working on a science project.

"How come?" Sophie continued. "No one ever goes to Upper Wappinger."

"We're looking for rocks," Violet said quickly, and turned to Thomas as if she were about to start an important conversation. Sophie didn't care. Subtleties were wasted on her.

"They have much better rocks down by the lake. Why aren't you going there?" Sophie persisted. "The rocks by the lake are older and much more interesting."

"Not to me," Thomas said.

"How can you say that?" Sophie asked indignantly.

"Some of the rocks in Upper Wappinger are at least ten thousand years older than the ones at the lake. They were formed in the early Mesozoic period." Thomas loved driving Sophie crazy, and he knew just how to do it.

By this time the bus had pulled up, and Thomas and Violet and McGrowl prepared to get on it. Thomas turned casually to Sophie and gave her one last factoid. "Many of the rocks in Upper Wappinger contain examples of the finest preserved fossils in the western hemisphere." Then he paid his fare, took a seat by the window, and waited for Sophie to explode.

Sophie looked up at him from the sidewalk. Her face was red, and she was trying desperately to think of something to say. She was not used to being at a loss for words. As the bus pulled away she called out to Thomas,

"Well, my grandmother found a diamond down by the lake once. And it was real. And I'm serious!" As the bus disappeared from view, Thomas could hear her screaming after it, "So there!"

Violet turned to Thomas. "Her grandmother never found anything at the lake. She was lying."

"So was I," Thomas replied, laughing. "There aren't any fossils in Upper Wappinger. I made the whole thing up." And then the bus turned down Lakefront Boulevard and headed for the bypass that would take them to the intersection of Willow Road and Round Swamp Lane. They would be at Wilbur Foote's house in less than fifteen minutes.

While the bus made its way over the winding roads to Upper Wappinger, Milton Smudge sat in his house on the wrong side of the tracks thinking his favorite thoughts. He thought about foreclosing mortgages on little old ladies' houses. He thought about taking candy from babies.

He was thinking about stealing books from the public library when he heard the insistent tinkling of a little bell. He reached into his pocket and took out what appeared to be a cell phone but was actually a tiny warning device. It signaled him whenever Thomas and McGrowl left their neighborhood. Smudge pressed a button, and a secret panel in the wall moved aside and revealed a television monitor.

The monitor was connected to a number of tiny cameras hidden in strategic places all over Cedar Springs. Thomas, Violet, and McGrowl didn't know it, but no matter where they went, they couldn't avoid the careful scrutiny of the evil duo.

"The fun's about to begin!" Smudge shouted.

"Goody, goody!" Bunting yelled in return as

she gleefully ran in from the garden. She had been pulling up flowers and planting weeds.

Smudge and Bunting watched the progress of the little bus as it chugged steadily onward. The pieces of their ingenious puzzle were falling nicely into place. *Soon it will all be ours,* Smudge told himself. *The dog. The world. Everything!* He rubbed his bony hands together gleefully.

Soon Smudge was halfway out the door, with Bunting close behind. "Wait for me!" she shouted.

"Fat chance!" he replied as rudely as ever. He disappeared around the corner and hopped into his nondescript car. Bunting hopped in right after him, and they sped off in the direction of their prey.

CHAPTER EIGHT
A-hunting We Will Go

Number 126½ Round Swamp Lane didn't seem to exist. Thomas found 126 Round Swamp Lane easily enough, and 127 Round Swamp Lane was right across the street.

"Maybe you wrote it down wrong," Violet suggested as the bus pulled away, leaving them alone on the deserted street.

"I'm sure that's what Maude Simple said," Thomas said as he checked the little piece of paper on which he had written the address. McGrowl looked around anxiously. Their only hope of finding Edwina rested in the hands of an ancient man who didn't appear to have a house.

And then McGrowl barked happily. He sent Thomas a telepathic message telling him to follow as he started walking toward an enormous thicket of weeds and brambles.

"Where are you taking us, McGrowl?" Thomas asked.

The golden retriever appeared to be leading them into an overgrown forest by the side of the house at 126 Round Swamp Lane. Cautiously, Thomas, Violet, and McGrowl approached the twisting vines and branches.

"Looks like Sleeping Beauty's castle without the castle," Violet said as she pulled burs from her jeans. McGrowl barked excitedly.

"I think he sees something," Thomas said as he fought his way through a mass of dense weeds that were nearly as tall as he was. Soon Violet lost sight of him altogether.

"Where are you?" she called.

"Over here," Thomas responded. Violet headed toward the sound of his voice. When she got there, she couldn't believe what she saw. In the middle of the thickest part of the foliage sat a tiny cottage. It looked as if elves lived there. It was impossible to tell where the tangle of green left off and the house began.

The roof was thatched, and the walls were made of mud and straw. A wizened face peered out through a little window. Thomas was attempting to locate the entrance. A bony hand pushed the window open, and a familiar voice shouted down at them, "Looking for the door? What are you, blind? It's as clear as the nose on your face."

And indeed it was. A minuscule sign with the numbers 126½ was hung beside a red-and-yellow door, right in front of McGrowl's substantial nose.

The door was only three feet tall. Thomas

had to stoop to enter. Violet followed close behind and so did McGrowl. There was barely enough space in the living room for the three of them.

The room was painted a faded yellow. It was furnished with a chair, a tiny sofa, and a lamp. The lampshade appeared to have been chewed on by tiny animals. This had indeed been the case. The house was teeming with mice and small birds that had turned the sofa into their personal nest.

Violet noticed immediately that newly laid eggs were tucked carefully into its corners (the faded cushions provided sufficient warmth for the chicks inside to develop happily). All in all, the house gave an impression that was not unfavorable.

"Sit down, have a cookie," a voice croaked. Thomas, Violet, and McGrowl looked up and saw a small, wrinkled man descending a staircase. The man pointed feebly in the direction of a plate of dusty-looking cookies sitting on the arm of the sofa.

Thomas concluded immediately that this was the cantankerous Wilbur Foote. He stood less than three feet tall, and he didn't walk, he crept. In fact, it appeared to require every ounce of his concentration to propel himself, shaking and spluttering, across the room.

Thomas and Violet held their hands out to greet him. Even McGrowl lifted a paw, but Wilbur Foote didn't notice. He was too busy edging his way toward the sofa.

The front door flew open and a voice rang out. "Whatever you do, don't eat those cookies, they're as old as he is!" The voice belonged to Maude Simple, and she was standing in the doorway tapping her foot and puffing furiously on a cigar.

Violet thought she seemed an unusual

choice for a caregiver. Maude looked every bit as old as Wilbur, and a little bit smaller. She did, however, appear to be more in control of her faculties than her employer. As Wilbur drew nearer to the sofa, she suddenly cried out, "Watch those eggs, they're about to hatch!"

Wilbur paid no attention as he fell into an exhausted heap on the couch. He immediately closed his eyes and began to snore. Miraculously, he had avoided breaking a single egg.

"Well, he might wake up in a few minutes, and then again, he might not," Maude Simple uttered matter-of-factly. Thomas wasn't sure whether she was suggesting that Wilbur had died or was merely taking one of his many naps.

The old woman bustled about the little kitchen and tended to a kettle that rested on top of a dilapidated wood-burning stove. The kitchen was as small as the living room and contained only the stove, a chair, and a small cupboard.

"Do you know where Edwina Tuttle lives, Miss Simple?" Thomas asked. Maude Simple stopped what she was doing and looked up at the ceiling as if the answer might suddenly appear there. When it didn't, she closed her eyes, scratched her head, and bit her lip. Her already severely wrinkled face appeared to fold in upon itself as she concentrated.

"We have to find her," Violet added. "It's really important."

"I'm not sure that I can help you there," the woman finally replied. She sighed as she unfolded her face. "I have a wonderful memory for everything but geography. I could tell you what I had for dinner three Mondays ago, but I'd be hard-pressed to tell you the name of the state we're living in."

"It's Indiana, Miss Simple," Thomas said.

"Funny, I could have sworn it was Iowa," she said, shaking her head. "Wilbur, on the other hand, can barely remember what his name is, but when it comes to addresses and locations, he's a regular phone book."

"That's wonderful, Miss Simple," Thomas said. McGrowl silently agreed. Their problem appeared to be solved. "So now all we have to do is wait for him to wake up."

"That's the ticket!" Maude smiled as she opened the cupboard and removed an exotic-looking tin box.

"Does Wilbur have any other living relatives, Miss Simple?" Violet asked.

"Depends on what you mean by living," Maude answered as she attempted to pry the lid off a can of tea leaves. "Can somebody give me a hand with this thing?" She waited while Thomas attempted to loosen the top. Then Violet gave it a try. Finally, McGrowl wandered over and took off the lid, using his teeth and paws. He had to pretend to struggle so that his bionic powers wouldn't be revealed.

After Maude carefully measured several teaspoons of the leaves and dumped them into the teapot along with a large dollop of honey and a pinch of oregano, she poured hot water into a beautiful but cracked china teapot. McGrowl had noticed the odor of oregano the moment he entered the cottage and was pleased to discover its source. Maude set the mixture aside to steep and began to speak.

"Edwina and Wilbur are cousins, you know. Those two were this close," Maude said, picking up two potatoes and smashing them together. One of the potatoes crumbled immediately into a mealy heap on the floor. One was so old it had hardened into a rocklike substance. It destroyed the other, newer potato on contact.

Several mice rushed over and ate the potato bits. "Don't fight, Eugene, there's plenty for everyone," Maude cautioned, wagging a finger at one of the larger mice. "He's actually quite delightful once you get to know him. But that's a mouse for you."

Thomas had to admit he didn't really know any mice.

"What a shame. Some of them have delightful personalities," Maude explained. "But you have to give them a chance to warm up to you. They can't be rushed."

The few remaining crumbs were eaten by a family of sparrows that lived under the eaves of the house. When they had finished, they flew onto Maude's head and shoulders and perched there peacefully.

Maude Simple poured the tea, sat down on the floor, and crossed her bony legs. She motioned for Thomas and Violet to do the same. She passed out mugs of tea to her guests and continued her story.

Maude had come to take care of Wilbur

Foote shortly after his wife died more than thirty years ago. "I had recently retired from being head nurse at Cedar General Hospital, and I needed a little something to do, so I answered Wilbur's ad in *Cedar Things.*

"My mom works for that paper," Violet said.

"I'm an avid reader," Maude said, her eyes lighting up. "What does she do there?"

"She writes a column called 'Mother Knows Best,'" Violet said proudly.

"Well, blow me over with a feather!" Maude exclaimed. "I love that column. I can't believe I'm sitting here drinking tea with Penny Schnayerson's kid. Wait till the girls in my poker game hear about this."

"Can you tell us anything else about Wilbur and Edwina, Miss Simple?" Thomas asked in an attempt to get the conversation back on track.

"Wilbur and Edwina were like brother and sister. You couldn't tear them apart. Until the big fight. But Edwina probably told you all about that," Miss Simple said as she reached up and poured everyone more tea.

"Actually, we've never really met, Miss Simple. My dog used to belong to her," Thomas said.

"Then you must be Alvin!" Maude Simple exclaimed, looking over at McGrowl. "I've heard so much about you."

McGrowl wagged his tail excitedly. "I'd like to shake your paw," Maude said, extending a bony hand. McGrowl offered his paw in return.

Just then Wilbur Foote appeared in the kitchen doorway, and Maude began to yell at him. "Tell us where Edwina Tuttle lives, Wilbur Foote!"

"What's that?" Wilbur asked, cupping his hands behind his ears. "Speak up. Can't hear a word you're sayin'."

"We're trying to find your cousin, Edwina

Tuttle!" Thomas hopped up and shouted directly into Wilbur Foote's ear.

"Well, why didn't you say so in the first place? The bathroom's out back behind the toolshed," Wilbur said, and then proceeded to snore loudly. He had fallen asleep standing up.

"Oh, that's not good," Maude said softly. "When he falls asleep standing up, he could be out for days. You kids have really exhausted him."

"We're very sorry, Miss Simple. Isn't there something you can do? We've simply got to find Edwina." As Violet spoke, McGrowl ran up to Wilbur Foote and barked loudly into his ear, to no avail.

"There is one thing . . ." Maude began. And she suddenly started darting about, clearing all the cups from the floor.

"We'll help with that, Miss Simple," Thomas volunteered.

"You can't. You might disturb the tea

leaves, and then I couldn't read your fortunes accurately," Maude said. She started lining everyone's cups carefully on top of the stove in preparation for the reading — even Mc-Growl's.

"But how will that help locate Edwina Tuttle?" Violet asked.

"If you're meant to find her, the leaves will tell us precisely where she is," Maude Simple replied mysteriously. And then she lit a candle, and the scent of lilacs filled the room.

"Remain very still. If I go into a trance, any loud noises could be extremely hazardous to my health," Maude said. Her eyes began to close, and she started murmuring an incantation. "Tea, tea, bring the truth to me, wherever you look, as far as you see . . ."

McGrowl sent Thomas a telepathic message. *What if she falls asleep, too?* he wondered. *Where will we be then?*

Maude Simple started to whirl around in a

tight little circle. Slowly at first. And then faster and faster.

Thomas was worried she would bump into the stove. Violet was concerned she might get dizzy. McGrowl worried that the spinning could kill her. At last, Maude stopped her twirling and gulped down the remaining liquid in the four cups of tea.

"I'm ready now," she said quietly. And then she wiped her mouth delicately with a tea towel and began to speak.

CHAPTER NINE

A New Leaf

".. . and Roger Wiggins will get eighty-six percent on his chemistry exam." Maude Simple sat down, exhausted from her reading. She had just finished Thomas's leaves, and she needed a breather. She fanned herself with a piece of cardboard and put her surprisingly large feet up on the stove.

"Those leaves don't know my brother very well," Thomas said, smiling. "He's never gotten more than seventy-five percent on anything."

"You mustn't question the leaves," Maude warned as she picked up McGrowl's cup and prepared to read his fortune. She had already finished Violet's, which foretold a visit from her Aunt Swoosie who lived in Peoria, and the pony that Violet had been wanting for her next birthday.

Violet had been impressed. Usually fortune-tellers made vague predictions for a pleasant year ahead or told you things you already knew, like "You are a natural leader." But Maude Simple's leaves were extremely specific.

"This is very unusual. What's going on here? Wait a minute . . ." Maude poked around in the bottom of McGrowl's cup. "What's that doing down there?" She reached in and plucked out a piece of birdseed one of the sparrows had dropped. "This won't tell us anything."

McGrowl leaned forward anxiously. He wanted to know if he was destined to meet up with Edwina. He missed her terribly. He was bursting to tell her all about his wonderful life with Thomas. He longed to be patted by her, and smell her lilac perfume, and find out how she was feeling. At last Maude spoke.

"I see a large brick building. I see a sign. I hear an ambulance. Edwina is upset. She misses Alvin. I see people in white outfits. Suddenly, everything is getting very dim." Thomas noticed that the lilac-scented candle was flickering as though it was about to go out.

McGrowl gave Thomas a worried look. Were the people in white outfits doctors from the hospital to which Edwina had been taken that fateful rainy Saturday afternoon? McGrowl remembered that day as if it were yesterday.

Edwina had been patting his head and telling him she would be all right. They would be at the hospital soon. And then all of a sudden, the ambulance they were in swerved to avoid hitting a squirrel, and the back doors flew open. As the driver careened back into his proper lane, McGrowl lost his footing and was thrown head over paws through the doors and out of the speeding vehicle.

The old woman could do nothing as the poor dog tumbled into the street and down the hill. "Alvin, come back!" she had cried weakly, but nobody heard her.

Maude spoke again. "You must go to that building. It is a hospital. There is a doctor there. He is very tall. He has one green eye and one brown one. He knows where Edwina lives. The hospital is very close to the corner of Sixth and Walnut. The leaves have spoken."

Suddenly, the candle went out and Wilbur opened his eyes. "It's *Eighth* and Walnut, ya dingbat. Stop all this gabbin' and make me a cup of tea." Then he fell back to sleep immediately.

Thomas and Violet thanked Maude Simple,

then hurried off with McGrowl to catch a bus to the hospital. It wasn't far, but, as McGrowl reminded Thomas, if they didn't hurry they wouldn't get home in time for Roger's basketball game.

A bus came quickly. They paid their fare and boarded. Soon they could see the hospital looming in the distance. The bus pulled to a stop, and Thomas and Violet and McGrowl got off. As they hurried down the street, they could see dozens of people streaming in and out of the hospital's large revolving doors.

They didn't notice the little gray cat running to catch up. She had lost McGrowl's scent at first but had managed to pick it up again after he left Wilbur Foote's. She couldn't wait to catch up to her savior. She had brought him a special present: a small mouse, wrapped neatly in a little brown paper bag. The mouse squeaked loudly, demanding to be let out.

Thomas, Violet, and McGrowl flew up the

enormous stairs that led to the hospital's entrance. Thomas and Violet were out of breath, but McGrowl wasn't even panting when an attendant stopped them. "Where do you think you're going with that animal?" he asked brusquely.

A large sign planted smack in the middle of the front door announced the hospital's policy in bold letters: NO ANIMALS ALLOWED. While the attendant turned to talk to someone else, Thomas and Violet checked out the possibility of sneaking in a side entrance. But every doorway to the building was either guarded or locked for security purposes.

Thomas glanced at his watch. They had to find the doctor and get to Edwina soon. Without warning, McGrowl took a couple of steps backward and crouched low to the ground. His powerful legs curled under him and suddenly unleashed a burst of energy that sent

GOOD DOG!

the dog flying into the air so quickly that nobody noticed a thing. Nobody, that is, except
Thomas and Violet. And, of course, the cat.
She purred admiringly at the sight of her
hero's amazing leap.

"Look at him go," Thomas whispered in
awe as McGrowl sailed thirty feet straight up
and into an open second-floor window. The
sudden gust of wind created by McGrowl's
powerful takeoff sent a nurse's cap flying. In
the back draft, a small boy visiting his mother
in the hospital lost the GET WELL SOON balloon
he was bringing her.

Thomas and Violet raced up the stairs and
through the revolving door. The attendant
nodded coolly and watched them closely, as
if they might have concealed a sixty-five-
pound golden retriever under their jackets. As
the cat attempted to dart into the building after them, the attendant closed the door soundly

in her face. He pointed angrily at the sign that forbade her admittance, as if she could read it.

McGrowl had flown through a second-floor window and landed in a laundry cart filled with used sheets. It was being pushed down the long hall by an overworked young nurse. The woman didn't notice anything out of the ordinary until McGrowl rose from the cart covered in a long white sheet, looking exactly like a ghost.

The terrified nurse let out a scream and ran down the hallway. She didn't look back. McGrowl shook himself loose from the sheet and began poking his nose discreetly into various rooms and closets, attempting to find the tall doctor who would lead him to Edwina.

Just then, a doctor left the nurse's station and strolled briskly in McGrowl's direction, peering down at a clipboard.

At that moment, Thomas and Violet turned

the corner and noticed that McGrowl was about to be discovered. Thomas grabbed a wheelchair and signaled the dog to hop on. The dog complied as Violet grabbed the sheet that had fallen to the floor and quickly wrapped McGrowl up in it.

Thomas took off his shoes and carefully arranged them so they poked out of the sheet and rested on the footrests at the bottom of the wheelchair. If you didn't look carefully, you might have thought that two dutiful children were wheeling around their aged grandparent, which is exactly what the doctor thought when he looked up from his paperwork. He wore a name tag clipped to his white coat: DR. ZUCKERMAN.

"Now, that's what I like to see," Dr. Zuckerman said enthusiastically. "How's Gramps doing?"

"Pretty well," Thomas said, looking up at

the doctor. A quick glance told him that the man was well over six feet tall.

"What's he in for?" the doctor asked as he took out a stethoscope and prepared to listen to McGrowl's chest.

Thomas mentioned the first thing that came into his head, which was appendicitis. Unfortunately, Violet mentioned the first thing that came into her head, which was pneumonia.

"Well, which one is it?" the doctor asked.

"Both," Thomas said quickly. "He came in to have his appendix removed. But then he got pneumonia."

"No wonder he looks so terrible. Let's have a better look," the doctor said as he leaned over and held up his stethoscope. As Dr. Zuckerman proceeded to examine him, McGrowl couldn't help but notice the man's unusual aftershave lotion. It smelled a lot like the tea Maude Simple had brewed.

Violet gave Thomas a nudge. She was close enough to the doctor to notice the color of his eyes. One was green and one was brown. There was no time to lose. At any moment, McGrowl could be discovered, and they would all be kicked out of the hospital.

"Do you know who Edwina Tuttle is?" Thomas ventured.

"Why do you ask?" the doctor replied, taking out a tongue depressor. "Say *ahhh*." McGrowl opened his mouth and did his best to say *ahhh*. It came out more like a whiny growl.

"We're trying to find her," Violet said. "Do you have any idea where she lives?"

"Yes, I do. She's a patient of mine," Dr. Zuckerman said as he peered into McGrowl's mouth. "Started coming here about a year ago. Lovely woman. You know, your grandfather has unusually large teeth."

"Really?" Thomas said, pretending to be

surprised. "I never noticed. Do you think you could give me her address? It's really important."

The doctor stopped what he was doing and turned abruptly to Thomas. "May I be completely honest with you?" he asked.

"Absolutely," Violet replied.

"Good, good," he murmured. "Well, there's no use beating around the bush. I'm thinking of ordering some tests for your grandfather. I don't like the way he looks."

McGrowl wasn't sure what the big fuss was about. He thought he looked perfectly fine.

"I'm not happy with his tonsils," the doctor continued. "And he seems to be suffering from a glandular disturbance of some kind. I don't want to worry you, but his nose is so huge it's off the charts. And I'm a little concerned about excessive facial hair."

"I never noticed," Thomas said innocently. "We're all pretty hairy in my family." The last thing he wanted was for McGrowl to undergo a series of tests. They'd never make it to Edwina's.

"It's true," Violet chimed in. "His Aunt Thelma practically has a full beard." As she spoke, Thomas started wheeling McGrowl down the hallway dejectedly. How would they ever find Edwina?

"I'll be back this afternoon," the doctor said. "We'll do some X-rays. Maybe a CAT scan."

They're not doing a cat scan on me, McGrowl thought.

"Won't hurt a bit," Dr. Zuckerman continued. "Tell your grandfather not to worry. He's lucky we caught it in time."

The doctor started walking away and then, realizing he had forgotten something, he turned back and whispered quickly: "Seventy-seven Whippoorwill Court. Go to the corner of Blue Jay Road and Nottingham Street and turn left.

You can't miss it. Doris and Buddy Wembley live there."

"Who are they?" Thomas asked, disappointed. The chances of finding Edwina seemed to be getting slimmer and slimmer.

"They're Edwina's best friends. They'll take you to her," the doctor said.

"Great," said Violet, relieved.

"Terrific," Thomas said, hoping this would be the last detour on the journey to find McGrowl's previous owner. Thomas was beginning to wonder if she really existed.

"And make sure your grandfather gets plenty of bed rest."

"Absolutely," Thomas said. He wheeled McGrowl away as quickly as he could.

"Push fluids!" the doctor yelled. By now, Thomas, Violet, and McGrowl were running for the back stairs. They had exactly three hours left to find Edwina and get Thomas home in time for the basketball game.

GOOD DOG!

The poor cat waited patiently in front of the hospital steps, still proudly carrying the mouse in the bag. She failed to notice McGrowl and his two human friends as they ran quickly out a back door and down the street.

CHAPTER TEN
Road to Nowhere

It wasn't hard to find the corner of Blue Jay Road and Nottingham Street, but after they turned left, Whippoorwill Court was nowhere to be seen. Once again, their search for Edwina threatened to end in failure. And then McGrowl detected the faint aroma of lilacs with his powerful nose and sent Thomas an immediate telepathic message. *Follow me.* He had picked up Edwina's scent and was off like a shot.

Soon the three travelers were running down a series of winding streets through a section of Upper Wappinger called the Heights. Thomas and Violet had never been here before. The streets were narrow and paved with cobblestones. They reminded Thomas of pictures he had seen once in a book about London.

There were clusters of quaint little shops with their colorful wares laid out on tables in front of storefront windows. Violet made a mental note to tell her mother about the area. It deserved at least a special mention, if not an entire column in "Mother Knows Best." If she hadn't been in such a hurry, Violet would have loved to spend some time browsing among the hats and clocks and antique whatnots she saw displayed everywhere.

The sun, which had been shining brightly all day, had moved behind some threatening storm clouds that had blown in from the east, and the wind had come up. A light rain began to fall.

Thomas pulled his collar up around his neck and wished he had brought along a hat. It was getting colder. Violet put her hands in her pockets and wished she had brought along the mittens her mother was always trying to get her to wear.

Thomas noticed the sign first: 77 WHIPPOOR-WILL COURT. It hung above the door of a brick-and-stone apartment building that stood four stories tall. McGrowl scratched on the door eagerly. It creaked loudly as Thomas pushed it open. He and Violet and McGrowl entered a small, dark corridor that led to the crumbling lobby of the building.

There were no windows. A single bulb dangling from a frayed cord provided the only illumination in the dim space. A layer of dust coated the few pieces of furniture that had been provided for visitors, and the walls were painted a dull green. *This must be what the past is like,* Thomas thought.

McGrowl barked softly and led Thomas and Violet over to a small desk on the far side of

GOOD DOG!

the lobby. As their eyes adjusted to the darkness, they could make out a strange-looking middle-aged woman seated behind the desk.

Horn-rimmed glasses accentuated her long, thin nose, and a hat with a large feather sat on top of her head. Closer inspection revealed she was busily filling out a number of forms that were piled haphazardly on the desk. She looked worried.

"What day is it?" she said to no one in particular. She hadn't noticed the three visitors.

"It's Saturday," Violet ventured, startling the woman.

"Ahhh!" She screamed as she lurched in her seat and looked up with alarm.

"You shouldn't sneak up on a person like that. It could give them a heart attack," the woman said, leaning over to pick up the pen that had flown out of her hand.

"We're sorry," Thomas said. "By any chance do Doris and Buddy Wembley live here?"

121

"I don't know. Let's have a look. I'm new."

Funny, she doesn't look new, Thomas thought. The woman looked as though she hadn't moved from behind the desk for the last twenty years. She started shuffling papers frantically. This caused a thick cloud of dust to rise, making the woman sneeze. Papers started flying off the desk.

"They might be under *B* for Buddy," the woman said as she sneezed again. *"Achoo!"* She reached up to grab a flying piece of paper.

"God bless you," Thomas said politely.

"Thanks so much," she replied, sneezing again. *"Achoo!"* She took out a handkerchief and started blowing her nose.

"God bless you, again," Violet said.

"Thanks ever so much," she replied. "But then again they might be under *W* for Wembley. It's hard to know. They could be under *D* for Doris for that matter. Or *T* for tenant, for all I know. Nobody ever puts anything away properly here. This is such a terribly run building. You might have noticed. I'm the manager, you know. But it's not really my fault. I'm new. I think I told you that. Esmerelda Snitch is the name," she said, holding out her hand grandly. Thomas wasn't sure if he was supposed to shake it or kiss it. He decided on the former. Miss Snitch proceeded to launch into a detailed history of the building.

As she spoke, Thomas and Violet and Mc-Growl were growing more and more impatient. At this rate they would be lucky to find Edwina by the time school started on Monday.

"Now, here's a piece of interesting information for you," Esmerelda said, holding up a yellowing document. "The first tenants moved into this building in 1912. I have the lease right here. And yet electricity wasn't installed until 1923. How do you like that?"

By now Violet had spotted a directory

posted on the wall behind her. After careful scrutiny she was able to locate WEMBLEY, BUDDY, THIRD FLOOR, APARTMENT H.

As Thomas, Violet, and McGrowl started running to the stairs, the woman called out to them. "You're not from the Department of Building Violations by any chance, are you?"

Thomas turned to the woman and shook his head no.

"That's a relief," she replied.

"Why?" Violet asked.

"You don't want to know," Esmerelda replied, and returned to the papers on her desk.

Thomas, Violet, and McGrowl made their way carefully up the stairs to the third floor. The banister was missing in several places, and an occasional rotting floorboard crumbled beneath their feet. They arrived on the third floor to find a tall woman wearing a sequined red dress and patent-leather high-heeled shoes skittering nervously down the hallway.

"Have you seen my rabbit?" the woman asked, eyeing Thomas and Violet suspiciously. Then she noticed McGrowl, who was sniffing around trying to pick up Edwina's lilac scent. The dust in the building seemed to be interfering with his superior powers of smell.

"You haven't eaten him by any chance, have you?" As she glowered at McGrowl, a small man in a tuxedo and a top hat came running down the hallway. He was panting heavily, and he dabbed at the beads of sweat that covered his forehead with a brightly colored silk scarf.

"It's okay, Doris, I've located the bunny." The man pulled a tiny lop-eared white rabbit from his jacket and gently held it up.

Thomas and Violet gave each other a meaningful look. If this was Doris, the man was likely to be Buddy. Edwina certainly had interesting friends. The man leaned over and stared into McGrowl's ear. The dog regarded him suspiciously.

A moment later the man spoke. "Kids, you gotta wash this dog's ears more frequently. Look what I found in there," he said as he began pulling an enormous collection of brightly colored cloths out of McGrowl's left ear. "And look what he's got in the other one." He pulled a realistic-looking rubber chicken out of the right one.

"This dog needs a bath," he proclaimed as he took what appeared to be a seltzer bottle out of his coat and started squirting it at McGrowl. McGrowl was alarmed at first, but he quickly noticed the bottle was filled with Silly String. After a few squirts, the man quickly turned the bottle itself into a beautiful bouquet of paper flowers. Thomas and Violet applauded enthusiastically. Even McGrowl was impressed.

"Doris and Buddy Wembley at your service," the man said, bowing deeply and making a grand gesture with his top hat. "What can we do for you?"

CHAPTER ELEVEN
Black Magic

"Now, hold very, very still," Buddy Wembley said as he lifted up a long, pointy sword and prepared to plunge it into a colorfully decorated large wooden box. Thomas was lying inside. Only his head could be seen, protruding from a small hole in the top. He was doing his best not to move.

"Wembley the Great must have absolute silence in order to perform this death-defying feat. I ask you to refrain from talking. I ask you to refrain from coughing. I ask you to refrain from breathing if you possibly can." The magician swirled his cape and paced about importantly as he spoke.

McGrowl watched apprehensively from the back of the living room. Violet was seated next to him on a small sofa. They remained motionless and as quiet as Maude Simple's mice.

The Wembleys' apartment didn't look like it belonged to two magicians. It was decorated tastefully and simply. Only a few large, colorful posters boldly announcing WEMBLEY THE GREAT AND THE AMAZING DORIS gave testimony to Doris and Buddy's line of work.

"One . . . two . . . three . . ." Buddy announced. Then he suddenly plunged the sword into the middle of the box with all his might. Thomas closed his eyes. McGrowl did, too. Violet watched through her fingers.

The sword went in a couple of inches and then struck what sounded like a dull metal object, causing it to break in two. Buddy muttered unhappily under his breath. Clearly a mistake had been made.

Meanwhile, Doris made a series of graceful gestures with her arms as she danced around in an effort to direct the viewers' eyes away from the box.

"We will take a brief intermission while Wembley the Great attempts to find out what went wrong. Perhaps the planets were not in alignment," Buddy said.

"Planets, my eye," Doris complained. "That trick hasn't worked since Denver. You're too cheap to buy a proper sword." With that, she turned on her high heels and stormed into the other room.

"Could somebody please let me out of here?" Thomas asked finally. "I've really got to find Edwina Tuttle."

"Well, why didn't you say so?" Buddy said. He unlatched the box and Thomas hopped out. Thomas decided it was useless to remind the magician it was the first thing he mentioned when he entered the apartment.

"Not long ago, Edwina was my assistant. That was before Doris," Buddy said as he tried unsuccessfully to glue the sword back together. McGrowl had a hard time picturing Edwina dancing around in a sequined red dress and high heels. He was also quite surprised to learn of her interest in magic.

"Wasn't she a little old?" Violet asked tentatively.

"She looked good from the back row. Listen, she was willing to do the matinees and she didn't eat very much. I don't ask a lot," Buddy grumbled.

"Well, you better go find her, 'cause this chicken's flyin' the coop," Doris said through clenched teeth as she stormed through the living room carrying a large suitcase and a coffeepot. "I've had it up to here." She made a gesture with the pot.

"Honey, think about the act!" Buddy wailed.

"I'm thinkin' about it. That's why I'm gettin' outta here!"

Thomas was desperate. It was nearly four o'clock, and he was no closer to finding Edwina than he was when he started. He looked to Doris. "Excuse me, ma'am, do you have any idea where I can find Edwina Tuttle? It's really getting late."

"What d'ya want with Winnie?" Doris asked, turning on her heels and striding back into the room. "That's Edwina's nickname."

With precious seconds ticking away, Thomas explained the story of McGrowl and Edwina Tuttle. He told the part about finding McGrowl in the ravine. He told the part about the daring cat rescue and McGrowl's appearance on TV. When he got to the part about Edwina's letter, Doris started to cry.

"I can't help it," she said, sniffling and blowing her nose. "Stories about dogs and cats and little boys and old ladies get me every time." She put down her suitcase and her coffeepot.

"Does this mean you're staying?" Buddy said hopefully.

"It sure does, ya big lug. We're gonna find Edwina. And we're gonna have one happy golden retriever on our hands." McGrowl got so excited he jumped onto Doris's lap and started licking her face. "Watch the eyelashes, blondie," she told McGrowl.

In minutes, the Wembleys, Thomas, Violet, and McGrowl were all on their way to find Edwina.

"I thought for sure she'd be here," Doris said as she exited Mae's House of Hair. "She's always having her hair done." *That's strange,* McGrowl thought. He didn't remember her ever having her hair done. There were a lot of things about Edwina he didn't seem to know.

She wasn't at the grocery store or the laundromat, either. "Oh, I know," Doris said, snapping her fingers. "She's probably at home, resting."

"You're right," Buddy said. "Why didn't I think of that?"

"That's why ya married me, ya dumb cluck!" Doris chuckled.

Looking for Edwina seemed to do wonders for their relationship, Thomas silently observed.

They walked for what seemed to Thomas like an eternity. It was raining harder now, and Buddy pulled an umbrella out of his sleeve and shielded the five of them as best he could.

Violet noticed there seemed to be a lot of uncollected trash in the alleyways. Thomas wondered why nobody in this part of town ever mowed their lawns. McGrowl wondered why Edwina would live in such a run-down neighborhood.

He also wondered why both Doris and Buddy Wembley smelled faintly like the tea Maude Simple had brewed. The hint of oregano tickled McGrowl's nose. It reminded McGrowl of Dr. Zuckerman's distinctive after-shave lotion.

And then McGrowl smelled the overpowering scent of lilacs and realized he was about to see Edwina. He reached up with one paw and tried to smooth down the hair on the top of his head. Edwina always said it looked like someone used an eggbeater on it. He was so happy he thought he would burst.

Thomas looked up and saw the house. A little sign on the door said E. TUTTLE, and a freshly painted white fence surrounded the only well-kept lawn in the neighborhood. Mc-Growl raced to the gate and waited patiently for Thomas to open it for him. He could have easily leaped over it, but he didn't want Doris and Buddy to notice his superpowers.

Thomas opened the gate, and McGrowl tried to contain his rising excitement. The lilac scent grew stronger as the five of them approached the front door. Even Thomas and Violet could smell it. *What has she done,* Thomas wondered, *sprayed the entire yard with her perfume?* The odor was, in a word, overpowering.

Doris knocked on the front door, and McGrowl started barking happily. *Will she still recognize my bark?* McGrowl wondered. His heart thumped wildly. In a moment, Edwina would be hugging him with her long bony arms and kissing his snout, the way she used to whenever she came back from a visit to the supermarket or the drugstore.

"That's funny, maybe she isn't home after all," Buddy said. He knocked harder on the door and it swung open silently, revealing an empty hallway that led to a darkened living room. McGrowl peered in. There wasn't a light on in the place, and although nothing appeared to be amiss, McGrowl knew immediately that something was very wrong.

The picture of Edwina on the wall that smiled down at him did nothing to reassure McGrowl. If anything, it made him more uneasy. Why would Edwina hang her own picture on the wall? It didn't make sense.

"Hello? Hello?" Thomas shouted. But no one answered back. The house seemed frightfully quiet. Something was definitely wrong.

Thomas and McGrowl and Violet exchanged uncertain looks as they started cautiously into the house. "I'll look upstairs. Why don't you look in the little room over there," Doris said happily as she practically skipped up the stairs. Buddy seemed unusually cheerful as well. "I'll look on the back porch.

She's probably taking a nap," he said, and bounced out of the room to take a look.

Why are they so happy? McGrowl wondered. And then in a flash he realized what was going on and sent Thomas an urgent message. *Danger! Get out! It isn't safe in this house!* He started pushing Thomas and Violet toward the front door and barking frantically.

In one last, desperate effort, McGrowl was able to shove Violet and Thomas out the door. Just then, every door and window in the house slammed shut with a tremendous crash. McGrowl barked loudly. Thomas recognized that bark. It meant McGrowl was scared and angry.

All at once, the whirring sound of a giant electromagnet starting up could be heard throughout the house, and McGrowl could feel the strength draining from his body. Soon he would barely be able to lift himself up, much less escape from the house. He was trapped. Thomas turned the knob and pushed frantically against the door, but nothing happened.

As McGrowl grew weaker and weaker, he realized that he had never encountered Edwina Tuttle's cousin Wilbur because Edwina didn't have a cousin Wilbur. And Wilbur wasn't Wilbur, anyway. Wilbur was Milton Smudge in another brilliant disguise, and so were Dr. Zuckerman and Buddy Wembley.

And Maude Simple wasn't that simple after all. She was Gretchen Bunting in disguise. And so was Doris Wembley. As well as Esmerelda Snitch, the woman in the lobby of the shabby apartment building.

And this most certainly wasn't Edwina's house. It belonged to Smudge and Bunting. The scents McGrowl had detected all day, like Maude Simple's tea and Dr. Zuckerman's aftershave lotion, had been used to cover the evil duo's tell-tale formaldehyde odor. The overpowering lilac smell was being used for the same purpose.

"No funny business or I'll punch you in the nose," Bunting said to McGrowl. She was still disguised as Doris Wembley as she tied up McGrowl and led him into the basement. She teetered on her shiny patent-leather high-heeled shoes. McGrowl was so weak he could barely lift his head.

Thomas had to get McGrowl back. His beloved pet had landed in the clutches of two of the most fiendish criminals in the world. There was no telling what they might do to him. Thomas looked at his watch. Five o'clock. He had one hour to rescue McGrowl, save the world, and return home, or he would have a lot of explaining to do.

CHAPTER TWELVE
Who Done It?

Still disguised as Doris and Buddy Wembley, Smudge and Bunting put a defenseless McGrowl in an electromagnetized trunk they had been keeping in the basement ever since they bought the house five short months before.

The crumbling house practically screamed "Fix me up!" But the evil duo didn't fix up the house at all. Instead, they worked day and night to install a tremendous network of electron-bearing wires throughout its moldy walls, creaky floors, and cracking ceilings. They set a trap for McGrowl inside the walls of a house from which no escape would be possible.

They were well aware that the only power on earth capable of rendering McGrowl helpless was generated by exactly the type of machine Smudge installed in the basement. The machine was connected to the wires that ran throughout the house.

Their plan was really quite simple: trap McGrowl inside the extensively wired house, turn on the electromagnet, and wait. "It'll be easy peezy lemon squeezy," Gretchen Bunting said. And she had been right.

The screens on the windows were specially wired. So was every door. So was every piece of furniture and every inch of wall and basement. It took months to install all that wiring. And it had been worth every minute. McGrowl was theirs.

Smudge began to laugh hysterically. What a perfect plan. Cunning in its simplicity. Why hadn't he thought of it before? He giggled until his sides ached and he doubled over and nearly lost his breath. Bunting got caught up in the merriment and began tickling her accomplice, who tickled her back even harder. As McGrowl lay, weakened, in his suitcase, Bunting yelled, "Uncle! Uncle!"

"Quiet!" Smudge snapped. The woman stopped immediately. "Someone's out there," he whispered frantically. "Check the monitors. I'll get the dog ready for transport."

While Bunting scanned the yard for suspicious activity, Smudge carried the trunk that held McGrowl into a tunnel underneath the basement floor. He put the trunk into a small motorized cart. The cart would carry the evil duo and their captive through a tunnel that wound its way underneath Cedar Springs to the outskirts of town, where a high-speed automobile was parked. It would take Smudge and Bunting along with McGrowl to their secret headquarters. From there, they would take over Cedar Springs, and soon, the world. Bunting had no idea where it was located. Only Smudge knew. And he wasn't telling anybody.

The doorbell rang loudly.

"Whoever it is, don't answer!" Smudge yelled to Bunting. It rang again. Bunting stared at the monitor in the basement, but she couldn't see who was ringing the bell. *Who could it be?* she wondered. *Doorbells don't simply ring themselves,* she thought. But there appeared to be no one there.

She tried to be good. She really did. But she didn't have much practice. She could restrain herself no longer. She had to see who was ringing that doorbell. She would be back before Smudge would even realize she had been missing.

The bell rang again. She raced upstairs to answer it. She threw open the door. An empty lawn stared back at her. "I know you're out there. You might as well show yourself," she called.

Still no one appeared. Bunting stamped her foot and shouted, "I'm counting to three, and if you don't tell me where you are I'll . . ." She paused as she tried to think of a really terrible threat. "I'll make you eat fried liver with nothing on it!"

Fried liver was about the worst thing Gretchen Bunting could think of to eat. But it happened to be the favorite food of her mysterious doorbell ringer. The cat who had been following McGrowl had been throwing herself desperately at the doorbell in a frantic attempt to get into the house. Each time she hit the bell, she would fall back onto the ground, preventing Bunting from seeing her.

Thomas and Violet had noticed the cat lurking nearby and had given her a gentle nudge in the right direction. Her nose had told her

MCGROWL

that her beloved rescuer was inside, and she was determined to see him and give him his mouse.

Suddenly, the cat came hurtling through Bunting's legs, and ran into the kitchen, looking for McGrowl. As she ran she lost her grip on the bag, and the mouse went flying up into Bunting's face. Terrified, it grabbed hold of the woman's nose. She danced wildly about, trying to shake it off.

Thomas and Violet, who had been hiding behind a garbage can, raced in through the open door, unnoticed, while Bunting struggled to dislodge the mouse.

By now, Smudge had loaded McGrowl's trunk into the cart. "All aboard," he shouted. "Last train leaves in thirty seconds." He meant business.

"Coming," Bunting yelled as she shook off the determined mouse and ran down the steps to the basement.

Meanwhile, Thomas and Violet ran into the kitchen to find the fuse box, while the cat followed Bunting into the basement. "You, get in here," Smudge barked at Bunting, who was struggling to get into the cart in high heels and tight red-sequined dress. "You, go away!" he yelled at the cat. She had picked up McGrowl's scent and was frantically sniffing around the basement.

Thomas and Violet struggled to remove the fuse that controlled the cart that was about to carry McGrowl off to a fate worse than death. It was stuck. They pushed and they pulled, but they were unable to budge it.

"Where's your rock?" Violet asked.

Thomas reached into his pocket. All he could find was the hole through which the magic rock his mother had given him had vanished. "It's not here."

"It's gotta be somewhere," Violet said urgently. "Look around."

Meanwhile, Smudge reached down to turn on the switch that would send the motorized cart catapulting through the tunnel. "One. Two. Three," he counted dramatically.

"Here it is!" Thomas shouted joyously. He had found the rock in the cuff of his pants. It had fallen through the hole in his pocket and gotten lodged there. He took the rock, and he pounded and pounded on the fuse. "I can't get it out."

"Maybe you can damage it," Violet suggested eagerly.

"It's worth a try," Thomas said, and he pounded harder.

"Nine. Ten," Smudge said grandly. "And we're off!" He flicked the switch. Instead of the expected *whoosh* of energy, the engine spluttered a few times, turned over, and then died.

"This is unacceptable," Smudge muttered. He got out and went upstairs to check the fuse box, leaving Bunting in the cart and the cat still searching the basement. When Thomas and Violet heard Smudge approaching, they hid behind a door. Smudge went into the kitchen to see what had happened to the fuse.

Just then, the mouse scampered into the basement. The cat spotted it, forgot about her hero, and started chasing madly after it. The mouse made a mad dash for what looked like safety and managed to run right into the middle of the giant electromagnet. The cat followed right behind.

Bunting shouted, "Bad cat!" at the top of her lungs. She took off her high-heeled shoes and attempted to throw them at the animal. Meanwhile, Smudge started back down the stairs.

"Some idiot smashed the fuse," he grumbled. Suddenly, the crackling sound of pulsating energy stopped as the electromagnet ground to a halt. McGrowl felt his powers slowly returning and prepared to turn the tables on his captors.

"I can't take it any longer," Smudge wailed. "What have I done to deserve this?"

"Well, first of all, you were a rotten child," Bunting began. "Second of all, you're not such a terrific adult. . . ."

"Oh, shut up!" Smudge hollered. He got on his hands and knees and crawled over to the electromagnet. "Come out, come out, wherever you are," he called to the cat. The cat wasn't interested in coming out — even to see McGrowl. She had saved McGrowl by disengaging the electromagnet. They were even. She no longer had to be nice to McGrowl. She had repaid her debt. If she ever found that mouse, she was keeping it. McGrowl would have to catch his own.

GOOD DOG!

Meanwhile, Thomas and Violet crept into the basement and snuck up behind Smudge.

Just then, McGrowl leaped out of the trunk and took Bunting by surprise. He tied her up and deposited her in the bottom of the cart just as Smudge turned around and noticed she was missing.

"Dddddd . . ." Bunting stammered from the bottom of the cart, trying to let Smudge know there was a bionic dog waiting to jump on him. "Dddddddd . . ."

"Enunciate," Smudge cried. "I can't understand a word you're saying."

As Bunting continued to stammer, Thomas softly whispered, "Yoo-hoo."

Smudge turned toward the boy. "What are you doing here, young man?"

"This," Thomas calmly replied, and gave Smudge a quick shove. The man tumbled into the cart. McGrowl jumped on Smudge and overpowered him while Thomas and Violet tied him up. In a moment, he was lying on the bottom of the cart, his evil partner by his side.

Then Thomas, Violet, and McGrowl grabbed on to the cart. McGrowl grasped it with his powerful teeth. They started pulling the cart through the tunnel.

Smudge and Bunting were stunned. Their perfect plan had failed. McGrowl and Thomas and Violet had won again.

Thanks to McGrowl's bionic powers, the three quickly pulled the cart through the maze of tunnels under Cedar Springs. McGrowl planned to drop Smudge and Bunting off at police headquarters and have Thomas and Violet home in plenty of time to get to Roger's basketball game.

As they reached the end of the tunnel, McGrowl looked in the bottom of the cart and all he could see was the bottom of the cart.

GOOD DOG!

Smudge and Bunting had escaped! Before devoting himself entirely to crime, Smudge had been an Eagle Scout. He had displayed an astonishing aptitude for knot tying. And untying.

As the cart sped through the darkened tunnel, Smudge had managed to loosen the knots that held him and Bunting captive. The evil duo had disappeared into the murky depths of the underground tunnel.

Thomas reached down and picked up a slip of paper. His hand shook as he read it: "'We'll be back. Just when you least expect us. You will not escape our evil plan. It's useless to try. Signed: Guess who.'"

Thomas and Violet hopped on McGrowl's back, and the dog carried them safely home. Smudge and Bunting were still on the loose, but Thomas and Violet were alive and well. And so was McGrowl. Thomas looked at his watch. It was exactly five-thirty.

CHAPTER THIRTEEN
Lilacs at Last

"And not a minute too soon, young man," Mrs. Wiggins chided as she watched Thomas and McGrowl walk up the front lawn. Violet had already been deposited at her parents'. "Where have you two been? You look like you've been out playing in a mudslide."

"We were," Thomas joked as he tousled the fur on top of McGrowl's head. McGrowl jumped up, licked Thomas's face, and knocked him over. The two of them wrestled and laughed until they lay on the lawn in an exhausted heap.

GOOD DOG!

"We have a surprise guest," Mrs. Wiggins said at last.

All of a sudden, McGrowl noticed the scent of lilac perfume. This one was fresh and clean. It smelled like real lilacs, not the artificial kind. It made his whiskers tingle. He looked up and saw Edwina Tuttle staring lovingly back at him.

Edwina had been thrilled to see her very own Alvin on Wally Flamm's television program that Monday evening. She didn't watch much television, but she never missed the six o'clock news. Edwina had recognized Alvin immediately and was relieved to find him alive and well. She wrote a letter to Thomas that very night and handed it to a friendly postal worker the very next morning.

But Thomas never got *that* letter. The friendly postal worker turned out to be none other than Gretchen Bunting posing as a mail carrier. She tucked Edwina's letter into her bag and ran gleefully home to show it to Smudge. Smudge was ecstatic.

Edwina's letter told Smudge and Bunting everything they needed to know in order to write their own, very different kind of letter. It was Smudge who did the actual writing. It was Bunting who came up with the ingenious idea of spilling a drop of water on Edwina's address.

The mysterious telephone number was Smudge's idea. He knew Thomas and Mc-Growl and Violet loved to play detective. He knew McGrowl would see the imprint on the envelope, and he knew Thomas would call the number. Smudge and Bunting were ready and waiting patiently in the tiny Foote cottage when Thomas called. Wilbur Foote didn't really exist, and neither did anyone else Thomas, Violet, and McGrowl encountered over the course of the day.

Why, you might ask, did the two evildoers

go to all the trouble of creating the elaborate worlds of Wilbur and Maude and Dr. Zucker-man? Why did they create the illusion of Doris and Buddy Wembley and Esmerelda Snitch, the strange apartment manager in the lobby?

Simple. If the letter led right to their final destination, someone could have followed them there. Thomas might have told his parents where he was going, and they could have shown up and ruined everything. Each beautifully set piece of the trap led to another finely tuned one. The whole plan was as precise as a seventeen-jeweled Swiss watch.

Meanwhile, the real Edwina waited for Thomas to answer the letter he never received. Now, Edwina was little, she was old, and she was a lady. But she wasn't a little old lady, and sitting around waiting patiently was not something she was likely to do for very long. When she didn't hear back from Thomas, she decided to take matters into her own hands and pay him a visit in person. She had hopped into her 1957 Chevy Impala, and two minutes later she was knocking on the Wiggins's front door.

Now Edwina Tuttle was standing in the doorway between Mr. and Mrs. Wiggins, holding a cup of tea in one hand and waving happily at McGrowl with the other.

She was dressed in her Sunday best. She had on the felt hat with the big artificial daisy McGrowl had come to know so well. She wore gloves and the well-worn tweed overcoat McGrowl had chewed on.

Her smile certainly was infectious. Thomas couldn't help returning the grin. Edwina's bright blue eyes twinkled behind wire-framed spectacles. Her round, rosy cheeks flushed with excitement as she looked at McGrowl.

Thomas held his breath as Edwina bent down to hug McGrowl. *Whatever happens,*

Thomas told himself, *I'll do what McGrowl wants. If he wants to go back to Edwina, he deserves to. And if she wants him back, it's only fair.*

McGrowl threw himself on the ground, and Edwina scratched his stomach. He brought her the Frisbee that Thomas had given him for his birthday and made her throw it for him. He rested his head on Edwina's lap and growled a growl of happiness when she patted down the unruly fur on the top of his head.

Then Edwina stood up and walked slowly over to Thomas. He held his breath. "He's yours now," she said. "When I saw the two of you playing together I realized I couldn't take Alvin away from you. And I couldn't take you away from Alvin. He's too happy. And so are you. You two belong together. It's as plain as the nose on your face. And in Alvin's case, that's saying a lot." She reached down and stroked his big nose gently. "I want you to promise me you'll all come and visit, though. It would mean a lot to me."

McGrowl sent Thomas a telepathic message. He told Thomas it would mean a lot to him, too. And he told Thomas how glad he was that Edwina had made the decision she made. He, of course, was happy to stay with Thomas.

Mrs. Wiggins said good-bye to Edwina and gave her a big goody basket to take home. It was filled with homemade scones, jellies, and gingerbread cookies in the shape of dogs. And then Mr. Wiggins had something to say. "Thank you for letting my son have your dog," he began. "He's a little large for my taste, and he barks too much. But I have to admit, he's a good dog."

And then Mr. Wiggins did an amazing thing. He turned to McGrowl and smiled. Again he said the words, "Good dog." McGrowl's heart leaped with joy. Then Mr. Wiggins presented Edwina with a number of Happy Tooth dental products. She didn't have the heart to tell him she had the kind of teeth you put in a glass beside the bed at night.

Edwina got in her car and drove away, and McGrowl ran down the street after her. He wagged his tail and barked until the car had turned the corner and was nearly out of sight.

All of a sudden, the cat McGrowl loved to hate came into view. She was walking across the street on the far side of the block. Mc-Growl couldn't help but growl. The cat looked over at him with an annoyed expression on her face. So far, so good.

McGrowl trotted over to her. She arched her back and hissed angrily. Even better. Mc-Growl broke into a full gallop. The cat was off and running.

McGrowl chased her until she reached the safety of the large maple tree that stood at the front of her lawn. As she scrambled up it, Mc-Growl debated following her. Thanks to his bionic powers, he could easily climb the tree with one paw tied behind his back if he wanted to. But he didn't want to. Not today. There would be other days, and other trees.

Then Thomas and the rest of the Wiggins clan got into the car and hurried off to watch Roger win his basketball game. McGrowl stayed home. He didn't mind. He was exhausted.

He considered going over to the Schnayersons' to see what Miss Pooch was up to. He considered digging a hole behind the bushes in the backyard where no one would see and hiding some old roast beef bones he had been saving in Thomas's closet.

He considered putting his head on his paws for just a minute. Before he knew it, he was fast asleep. He dreamed of lilacs and tweed overcoats. He dreamed of Thomas and their most recent exciting adventure. He dreamed of a day when Milton Smudge and Gretchen Bunting were behind bars and the world was a safer place.

Photography: Lee Salem

Bob Balaban is a respected producer, director, writer, and actor. He produced and costarred in Robert Altman's Oscar®- and Golden Globe–winning film *Gosford Park*, which was named Best British Film of 2001 at the British Academy Awards. He appeared in *Close Encounters of the Third Kind*, *Absence of Malice*, *Deconstructing Harry*, *Waiting for Guffman*, *Ghost World*, *The Mexican*, and *A Mighty Wind*, among many other films, and appeared on *Seinfeld* several times as the head of NBC. Bob produced and directed the feature films *Parents* and *The Last Good Time*, which won best film and best director awards at the Hamptons International Film Festival. Bob lives in New York with his wife, writer Lynn Grossman, and his daughters, Hazel and Mariah. At the moment, he is canine-less, but he is looking forward to a close encounter with his own actual dog, not just one of the literary kind.

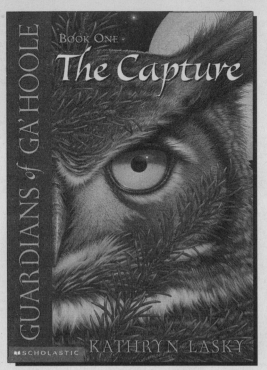